DEATH OF
AN
OUTSIDER

The Hamish Macbeth series

DEATH OF AN OUTSIDER

A Hamish Macbeth Murder Mystery

M. C. Beaton

Constable & Robinson Ltd
55–56 Russell Square
London WC1B 4HP
www.constablerobinson.com

First published in the USA by St Martin's Press, 1988

First published in the UK by Robinson,
an imprint of Constable & Robinson Ltd., 2008

This edition published by C&R Crime,
an imprint of Constable & Robinson Ltd., 2013

A copy of the British Library Cataloguing in
Publication Data is available from the British Library

ISBN: 978-1-47210-522-6 (paperback)
ISBN: 978-1-78033-204-8 (ebook)

Printed and bound in the UK

1 3 5 7 9 10 8 6 4 2

FOR THE LAIRG VOLUNTEER FIRE
BRIGADE . . . GOD BLESS 'EM

Sub-Officer	John Corbett
Leading Fireman	Archie Fraser
Leading Fireman	Willie McKay
Fireman	William Ross
Fireman	Michael Corbett
Fireman	Duncan Matheson

Hamish Macbeth fans share their
reviews . . .

'Treat yourself to an adventure in the Highlands;
remember your coffee and scones – for you'll want
to stay a while!'

'I do believe I am in love with Hamish.'

'M. C. Beaton's stories are absolutely excellent . . .
Hamish is a pure delight!'

'A highly entertaining read that will have me
hunting out the others in the series.'

'A new Hamish Macbeth novel is always a treat.'

'Once I read the first mystery I was hooked . . . I
love her characters.'

Share your own reviews and comments at
www.constablerobinson.com

Chapter One

See, the happy moron,
He doesn't give a damn,
I wish I were a moron,
My God! Perhaps I am!
– Anonymous

Constable Hamish Macbeth sat in the small country bus that was bearing him away from Lochdubh – away from the west coast of Sutherland, away from his police-station home. His dog, Towser, a great yellowish mongrel, put a large paw on his knee, but the policeman did not notice. The dog sighed and heaved itself up on to the seat beside him and joined his master in staring out of the window.

The bus driver was new to the job. 'Nae dugs on the seats,' he growled over his shoulder, determined not to be intimidated by Hamish's uniform. But the constable gave him a look of such vacant stupidity that the driver, a Lowland Scot who considered all

Highlanders inbred, decided it was useless to pursue the matter.

Misery *did* make Hamish Macbeth look dull-witted. It seemed as if only a short time ago he had been happy and comfortable in his own police station in Lochdubh, and then orders had come that he was to relieve Sergeant MacGregor at Cnothan, a crofting town in the centre of Sutherland. In vain had he invented a crime wave in Lochdubh. He was told that protecting the occasional battered wife and arresting a drunk once every two months did not amount to a crime wave. He was to lock up the police station and go by bus, for Sergeant MacGregor wished his stand-in to keep his car in running order.

Hamish hated change almost as much as he hated work. He had the tenancy of some croft land next to the police station at Lochdubh, where he kept a small herd of sheep, now being looked after by a neighbour. He earned quite good money on the side from his small farming, his poaching, and the prize money he won for hill running at the Highland Games in the summer. All that he could save went to his mother and father and brothers and sisters over in Cromarty. He did not anticipate any easy pickings in Cnothan.

Crofters, or hill farmers, always need another job because usually the croft or smallholding is too small a farm to supply a livelihood. So crofters are also postmen, forestry workers, shopkeepers, and, in the rare case of Hamish Macbeth, policemen.

It was the end of January, and the north of Scotland was still in the grip of almost perpetual night. The sun rose shortly after nine in the morning, where it sulked along the horizon for a few hours before disappearing around two in the afternoon. The fields were brown and scraggly, the heather moors, dismal rain-sodden wastes, and ghostly wreaths of mist hung on the sides of the tall mountains.

There were only a few passengers on the bus. The Currie sisters, Jessie and Nessie, two spinster residents of Lochdubh, were talking in high shrill voices. 'Amn't I just telling you, Nessie?' came the voice of Jessie. 'I went over to the Royal Society for the Prevention of Cruelty to Animals at Strathbane last week and I says to the mannie, "I want a humane trap to catch the ferret that has been savaging our ducks." He gives me the trap, and he says, "You take this here humane trap, and you humanely catch your ferret, and then, if you want my advice, you will humanely club the wee bastard to death." Sich a going-on! And him supposed to be against cruelty. I have written to our Member of Parliament to complain most strongly.'

'You told me a hundred times,' grumbled Nessie. 'Maybe he was right. For all you caught in that humane trap was the minister's cat. Why don't you tell Mr Macbeth about it?'

'Him!' screeched Jessie. 'That constable is a poacher and it was probably his ferret.'

The bus jerked to a halt and the sisters alighted, still quarrelling.

Three months in Cnothan, thought Hamish, absent-mindedly scratching Towser behind the ears. They say Lochdubh is quiet, but nothing ever happens in Cnothan, and nothing ever will. Did I not have the two murders in Lochdubh?

He thought of the murder that had taken place last summer and how it appeared to have brought him closer to the love of his life, Priscilla Halburton-Smythe. But Priscilla, the daughter of a local landowner, had then left, just before Christmas, to go to London to find work. She never stayed away for very long. She might even be heading north now, and would return to Lochdubh to find him gone.

'And she will not be caring one little bit!' said Hamish suddenly and loudly. The bus driver bent over the wheel and congratulated himself on his decision to leave this crazy copper alone.

Hamish knew Cnothan and thought it must be the dullest place in the world. Although designated a town, it was about the size of a tiny English village. He remembered the inhabitants as being a close, secretive, religious bunch who considered anyone from outside an interloper.

At last, he was the only passenger left on the bus. The bus lurched and screeched around hairpin bends, finally racing out of the shadow of the tall pillared mountains to plunge down into the valley where Cnothan stood, in the middle of Sutherland.

Hamish climbed down stiffly and collected his belongings, which were packed into a haversack and an old leather suitcase. The bus departed with a roar and Hamish pushed his peaked hat back on his fiery hair and looked about him.

'High noon in Cnothan,' he muttered.

It was the lunch hour, which meant all the shops were closed and the main street was deserted. A savage wind screamed down it. Not even a piece of scrap paper was borne on the wind. The town had a scrubbed, grey, antiseptic look.

Cnothan stood on the edge of an artificial loch caused by one of the ugliest hydroelectric dams Hamish had ever seen. What you saw was what you got. There were no quaint lanes or turnings. One straight main street led down to the loch. There were four grocer's shops, which all sold pretty much the same sort of goods, a hardware, a garage, a craft shop, a hotel, a fish-and-chip shop, a butcher's, a pub, and an enormous church.

The government-subsidized housing was tucked away on the other side of the loch, segregated from Cnothan's privately owned houses, which were all very small and drab and looked remarkably like the government ones.

The town was so barren, so empty, it reminded Hamish of scenes in a science-fiction movie he had once seen.

And yet he was aware of eyes watching him, eyes hidden behind the neatly drawn lace curtains.

He opened the garden gate of the bungalow nearest him, called Green Pastures, and went up and rang the brass ship's bell that hung outside the door. Silence. A plaster gnome stared at him from the garden and the wind moaned drearily.

A mail-order magazine protruded from the rubbish bin beside the door. Hamish twisted his head and read the name on it. Mrs A. MacNeill. At last he heard footsteps approaching. The door was opened a few inches on a chain and a woman's face peered through the crack, one of those sallow Spanish types of faces you find in the Highlands of Scotland.

'What is it?' she demanded.

Now Hamish knew in that instant that the woman knew exactly who he was. Her manner was too calm. For in a relatively crime-free area, the arrival of a policeman on the doorstep usually creates terror because it means news of a death or accident.

'I am Constable Macbeth,' said Hamish pleasantly, 'come to replace Mr MacGregor who is going on holiday. Where is the police station?'

'I dinnae ken,' said the woman. 'Maybe it's up the hill.'

'At the top of the main street?' asked Hamish. He knew the woman knew perfectly well where the police station was, but Hamish was an incomer, and in Cnothan, you never told incomers anything if you could help it.

'It could be, but why don't you ask someone else?' said the face at the door.

Hamish leaned against the door jamb and studied the sky. 'Aye, it iss blowing up,' he said in his soft Highland voice, which became more sibilant when he was angry or upset. 'Now, Mr MacGregor, he will be going to Florida to visit his brother, Roy. It will be hot there this time of year.'

'Aye, it will,' said the woman.

'And I call to mind he has the sister in Canada.'

The chain dropped and the door opened another few inches. 'That's Bessie,' said the woman. 'Her that is in Alberta.'

'True, true,' agreed Hamish. 'And you are Mrs MacNeill?'

'Now, how did you ken that?' asked Mrs MacNeill, opening the door wide.

'Oh, hass not everyone heard of Mrs MacNeill,' said Hamish. 'That's why I called. People are not often anxious to give directions, but I said to myself, that Mrs MacNeill, being a cosmopolitan sort of lady, would help if she could.'

Mrs MacNeill simpered awfully. 'You are asking about the police station. Yes, as I was saying, it is right at the top of the main street on the left. They are packed and ready to leave.'

'Thank you.' Hamish touched his cap and strolled off. 'Cantankerous auld bitch,' he muttered to Towser, 'but there was no point in asking anyone else, for I suppose they'll all be the same.'

At the top of the main street was a long, low, grey bungalow with the blue police lamp over an extension to the side. A small angry police sergeant was striding up and down outside.

'What kept ye?' he snapped. And then, before Hamish could open his mouth, he went on, 'Come in. Come in. But leave that dog outside. There's an old kennel at the back. It can sleep there. No dogs in the house.'

Hamish told Towser to stay and followed the sergeant into the house. The sergeant led the way through to the extension. 'Here's the desk, and don't you mess up my filing system. And there's the keys to the cell. You'll have trouble wi' Sandy Carmichael of a Saturday. Gets the horrors something dreadful.'

'If a man has the DTs, isn't it better to get him to the hospital?' asked Hamish mildly.

'Waste o' public money. Jist strap him down on the bunk and let him rave away until morning. Come ben and meet the wife.'

Hamish loped behind the bustling policeman. 'She's in the lounge,' said Sergeant MacGregor. Mrs MacGregor rose to meet them. She was a thin, wispy woman with pale eyes and enormous red hands. Hamish's pleasantries were cut short.

'I like to keep the place nice,' said Mrs MacGregor. 'I don't want to come back from Florida and find the place like a tip.'

Hamish stood with his cap under his arm, his hazel eyes growing blanker by the minute. The living-room in which he stood, which had been exalted to a lounge by the MacGregors, was a long, low room with pink ruched curtains at the windows. A salmon-coloured three-piece suite, which looked as if it had been delivered that day, stared back at him in all its nylon velveteen overstuffedness. The walls were embellished with highly coloured religious pictures. A blond and blue-eyed Jesus suffered the little children to come unto him, all of them dressed in thirties school clothes

9

and all of them remarkably Anglo-Saxon-looking. A carpet of one of the more violent Scottish tartans screamed from the floor. There was a glass coffee-table on wrought iron legs in front of the sofa, and a glass-and-wrought iron bar stood in one corner, with glass shelves behind it lit with pink fluorescent strip lighting and containing, it seemed, every funny-looking bottle ever invented. An electric heater with fake logs stood in the fireplace. In the recesses of the room were glass shelves containing a startling variety of china ornaments: acid-green jugs in the shape of fish, little girls in pastel dresses holding up their skirts, bowls of china fruit, dogs and cats with Disney smiles on their highly glazed faces, and rows of miniature spun-glass objects, of the type of spun glass you see at fairgrounds. On a side table lay a large Victorian Bible, open at a page where there was a steel engraving of an epicene angel with scaly wings throwing very small anguished people in loincloths down into a fiery pit.

Mrs MacGregor then led him from one frilly overfurnished bedroom to another. The bungalow boasted five.

'Where's the kitchen?' asked Hamish, finding his voice.

She trotted on her high heels in front of him, head down, as if charging. 'In here,' she said. Hamish stifled a sigh of relief. The kitchen was functional and had every labour-saving device imaginable. The floor was tiled, and there was a good-sized table. He decided to shut off that terrible lounge for the duration of his stay.

'Have you got television?' he asked.

Mrs MacGregor looked up at the tall, gangling policeman with the fiery-red hair and hazel eyes. 'No, we don't believe in it,' she said sharply, as if debating the existence of little green men on Mars.

'I see you have the central heating,' remarked Hamish.

'Yes, but we have double glazing on the windows, so you'll find you hardly need it. It's on a timer. Two hours in the morning and two in the evening, and that's enough for anyone.'

'Well, if I could chust haff a word with your good man . . .' began Hamish, looking around for the police sergeant, who had disappeared during the tour of the house.

'There's no time, no time,' she said, seizing a bulging handbag from the kitchen counter. 'Geordie's waiting with the taxi.'

Hamish looked at her in amazement. He wanted to ask MacGregor about duties, about where the keys to the car were kept, about how far his beat extended, about the villains of the parish. But he was sure the MacGregors were cursed with what he had rapidly come to think of as Cnothanitis: Don't tell anyone anything.

He followed her out to the taxi. 'So you'll be away three months, then?' said Hamish, leaning on MacGregor's side of the taxi. The sergeant stared straight ahead. 'If you'd get out of the road, Constable,' he said, 'we might be able to get to the train on time.'

'Wait a bit,' said Hamish. 'Where are the keys to your car?'

'In it,' snapped MacGregor. He nodded to the taxi driver and the cab moved off.

'Good riddance,' grumbled Hamish. He jerked his head to Towser, who followed him into the kitchen. Hamish took the central heating off the timing regulator and turned up the thermostat as high as it would go and started to examine the contents of the kitchen cupboards to see if there was any coffee. But the cupboards were bare; not even a packet of salt.

'You know, Towser,' said Hamish Macbeth, 'I hope they get hijacked to Cuba.'

He went through to the office and examined the files in a tall filing cabinet in the corner. It was full of sheep-dip papers and little else. Not dipping one's sheep seemed to be considered the major criminal offence in Cnothan. There came a crashing and rattling from the kitchen. He ran through. Towser had his large head in one of the bottom cupboards, which Hamish had left open, and was rummaging through the pots and pans.

'Get out of it, you daft animal,' said Hamish. 'I'll just away to the shops and see if I can get us some food.' He searched until he found a bowl and filled it with water for the dog. Then he ambled out of the house and down the main street. The lunch hour was over and the shops were open again. People were standing in little knots, gossiping, and as he passed, they stopped talking and stared at him with curious and unfriendly eyes.

He bought two bags of groceries and then made his way down to the garage, which also sold household goods. He asked if he could rent a television set and was curtly told by a small man whose face was set in lines of perpetual outrage that no, he could not. To the shopkeeper's irritation, Hamish did not go away, but kept repeating his question in a half-witted sort of manner, looking around the other customers as he did so.

A small, thin, birdlike woman with sharp features came up to him. 'You will be Mr MacGregor's replacement,' she said briskly. 'I am Mrs Struthers, the minister's wife. Can we expect to see you at church on Sunday?'

'Oh, yes,' said Hamish amiably. 'My name's Macbeth. I am a member of the Free Church myself.' Hamish had taken careful note of the denomination of Cnothan's main church. He was not a member of the Free Church, or, indeed, of any other church.

'Well, that's splendid!' cried Mrs Struthers. 'Now, I heard you asking about a telly. We have a black-and-white one we are going to raffle at Easter. I could lend you that.'

'Very kind of you,' said Hamish, smiling down at her. That smile changed his whole face. It was a smile of singular sweetness.

In no time at all, Hamish was resting his boots on a footstool in the manse and being plied with tea and scones.

'I am thinking, Mrs Struthers,' said Hamish, 'that it will be a wee bit difficult for me here. They never did like incomers in Cnothan.'

'Well ...' said Mrs Struthers cautiously, going to the window to make sure there was no sign of her husband returning from his rounds, her husband having preached about the iniquities of gossip the previous Sunday, 'people here are very nice when you get to know them. All it takes is a few years.'

'I haven't got the time,' said Hamish. 'I'm only here for three months.'

'They'll come around quicker,' she said, 'because they're all united against a really nasty incomer.' She looked around and her voice dropped to a whisper. 'An Englishman.'

'Oh dear,' said Hamish encouragingly. 'They do not like the English?'

'It's not that,' said the minister's wife. 'It's just he's such a know-all. It's a crofting community round here. They don't like being told how to run things, particularly by an outsider, but Mr Mainwaring, that's his name, *will* tell them what they are doing wrong. Not in a nasty way, mind. But as if he's laughing at them. His poor wife. He won't even leave her to run the house, but supervises her cooking. He even *chooses her clothes* for her!'

'The fiend!' cried Hamish, registering extreme shock, very gratifying to the minister's wife, who had not had such an appreciative audience in years.

'Have another scone, Constable. Yes, she is a member of the Women's Rural Institute and gave us a very good lecture on how to dry and arrange flowers. Most stimulating. She was doing very well, but he walked in at the question time and started grilling her – his own wife!'

'Fancy!'

'Yes. And she turned as red as fire and began to stammer. Wicked it was. And . . .'

The sound of a car crunching on the gravel outside made Mrs Struthers turn as red as fire herself. 'I had better go,' said Hamish, not wishing to waste time talking to the minister.

But as he rose to his feet, Mr Struthers, the minister, came in. He had a pale face and pale-blue eyes and a thin mouth. His tow-coloured hair was carefully sleeked down. Mrs Struthers, rather flustered, made the introductions. 'I trust you have not been gossiping,' said the minister severely.

'On the contrary,' said Hamish, 'your good lady has just been encouraging me to visit the kirk on the Sabbath. She was telling me all about your powerful sermons.'

He shook hands with the minister, collected the small television set, and said goodbye. The minister's wife went to the window and watched the tall figure of the constable as he walked away with a rather dreamy smile on her face. 'Such a fine man,' she murmured.

Hamish ambled up the main street, comfortably full of tea and home-made scones and jam. At the top, opposite the police station, he noticed an old cottage, set a little back from the road, with a sign outside which said, PAINTINGS FOR SALE.

There was what appeared to be a teenage girl digging the garden. As if aware she was being watched, she turned around, saw Hamish, and came up to the garden gate. Her figure was as trim and youthful as a girl's, but Hamish judged her to be about the same age as himself – in her thirties. She had an elfin face, a wide smile, and a mop of black curls.

'Jenny Lovelace,' she said, holding out a small, earthy hand.

'Hamish Macbeth,' said Hamish, smiling down at her. 'Is that an American accent?'

'No, Canadian.'

'And what are you doing in the wilds of Sutherland, Miss Lovelace?' asked Hamish, putting down the television set and two grocery bags on the ground and shaking her hand before leaning comfortably on the gate.

'I wanted peace and quiet. I came over on a holiday and stayed. I've been here four years.'

'And do you like it? I gather they don't like incomers here.'

'Oh, I get along all right. I like being alone.'

'I get the idea life has been easier for the incomers since a certain Mr Mainwaring arrived. He sounds like a right pain in the neck.'

Jenny's face hardened. 'Mr Mainwaring is about the only civilized person in the whole of this place,' she said sharply.

'I always go and put my big foot in it,' said Hamish sadly. 'It comes from not being in the way of talking to pretty girls. My mind gets all thumbs.'

Jenny giggled. 'Your mind doesn't have thumbs,' she said. 'Gracious! What's that terrible howling coming from the police station?'

'It's my dog, Towser. He wants his food, and when he wants his food, he screams for it. I'd best be on my way.'

'Drop round for a coffee,' said Jenny, turning away, as Hamish stooped to pick up his belongings.

'When?' Hamish called after her.

'Any time you like.'

'I'll drop by the morn,' called Hamish, feeling suddenly happy.

Towser's howling stopped when he saw his master. He lay on the kitchen floor and stared at Hamish with sorrowful eyes. 'I've got some liver for ye,' grumbled Hamish, pouring oil in a pan. 'See, low cholesterol oil, good for your fat heart.' The doorbell on the police-station extension sounded shrilly. Hamish made a move to answer it. Towser started to howl again.

Hamish ran and wrenched open the door. A middle-aged man stood on the step. He was tall, well-built, and had a large round head and neat prim features, small round eyes, a button of a nose, and a small primped mouth. Although he must have been nearly sixty, he had a thick head of brown hair, worn long so that it curled over his collar. He was wearing a waxed coat with a corduroy collar, gabardine breeches, lovat stockings, and brogues – and a red pullover. English, thought Hamish. They aye love thae red pullovers.

'Come in and I'll be with you in a minute,' gabbled Hamish as Towser's howling rose to a crescendo. Hamish darted back to the kitchen and put the liver in the frying pan. When it was ready, he cut it up into small pieces, arranged it on a dish, and put it in front of the dog.

'So we've lost one fool of a policeman to find another,' said a sarcastic upper-class-accented voice from the doorway of the kitchen. 'Let me tell you, Constable, that I am going to write to your superiors and say that feeding good butcher's meat to a spoilt mongrel takes precedence in what's left of your mind over solving crime.'

'Sit yerself down, Mr Mainwaring,' said Hamish, 'and I'll attend to you. I havenae had time to draw breath since I arrived.'

'How do you know my name?'

'Your reputation goes before you,' said Hamish. 'Now, we can stand here exchanging insults or we can get down to business. What's the crime?'

William Mainwaring drew out a kitchen chair and sat down and looked up at the tall policeman. He took out a pipe and lit it with precise, fussy movements. Hamish waited patiently.

'You ask me what the crime is?' said Mainwaring finally. 'Well, I'll tell you in one word:

'Witchcraft.'

Chapter Two

There's one parish church for all the people,
whatsoever may be their ranks in life or their
degrees,
Except for one damp, small, dark, freezing cold,
little Methodist chapel of ease,
And close by the churchyard there's a
stonemason's
yard, that when the time is seasonable.
Will furnish with afflictions sore and marble
urns
and cherubims very low and reasonable.
                                    – Thomas Wood

'Witchcraft,' said Hamish Macbeth. 'Jist let me get my notebook.' He licked the end of his pencil and looked with delighted curiosity at William Mainwaring.

'Yes, witchcraft,' said Mainwaring testily. 'Last week, I found crossed rowan branches placed outside the door. I am an expert on local folklore and knew this was to put a hex

21

on us. Two days later, I found fingernails – the same thing. Then, last night, my wife was making her way home from the Women's Rural Institute when three witches jumped over the churchyard wall and started cackling and howling about her.'

Hamish bit the end of his pencil thoughtfully. 'Who is it that wants to drive you away?' he asked.

'Oh, everyone, I should think,' said Mainwaring.

'And why is that?'

'Because we are incomers and English.'

'And nothing else?'

'No other reason whatsoever,' said Mainwaring. 'I am by way of being a leader of the community. They are a simple people here and look to me for guidance. It should be easy for you to find out the culprits and arrest them.'

'But if you are a leader of the community and looked up to,' asked Hamish blandly, 'then why do they want to get rid of you?'

'We're English, that's all. And you don't expect rational behaviour from these people. Also, the attack was directed against my wife. She is probably the target, now I come to think of it. She is a highly irritating woman.'

Hamish blinked. 'In that case,' he said, 'perhaps it would be better if I had a wee word with Mrs Mainwaring.'

'Agatha has nothing to tell you that I cannot.

You will probably find it is some of those bitches at the Women's Rural Institute. I attended one of my wife's lectures, and I could feel the atmosphere was hostile.'

'And at what time did this take place last night?'

'At ten o'clock, or as near as damn.'

Hamish looked at his shorthand notes. 'Why did you not report the matter to Sergeant MacGregor?'

Mainwaring laughed. It was a pleasant and charming laugh, at odds with the words that followed. 'MacGregor is a fool, and I have had reason to complain about him to his superiors on two occasions. I knew you, his replacement, would be arriving today and decided I would be better with fresh blood. You do not appear particularly intelligent to me, but, with my guidance, I should think we might get somewhere. I have experience of this sort of thing.'

'Witchcraft?'

'No, no, man. Detective work. Did my bit in the army. Not supposed to talk about it, but the little grey men in Whitehall called me in from time to time to ask my help.'

'And do you often talk to little grey men?' asked Hamish, deliberately misunderstanding him.

'God give me patience,' cried Mainwaring, his face turning a mottled colour. 'M.I.5, you fool!'

'Is that a fact!' exclaimed Hamish, his eyes round with wonder. 'Aye, I can see we'll have your witches in no time at all, at all, with a brain like yours to help with the work.'

'You can start off with Mrs Struthers, the minister's wife. She runs the local WRI,' said Mainwaring.

'How long have you been in Cnothan?' asked Hamish.

'Eight years.'

Hamish was not in the least surprised that someone who had been in Cnothan for eight years was still regarded as an outsider. 'And why did you come here?'

'My aunt was Scottish. She left me the house and the croft in her will. I like fishing and hill walking. I am a crofter, of course. I have two hundred Cheviots.'

Hamish stared blankly ahead. In his experience, incomers were often misguided romantics who thought they could get away from their troubles by leading a simple life in the Highlands of Scotland. They often took to drink. But there was no sign of the drinker about Mainwaring. Hamish wondered whether, as a retired army man in Chelmsford or somewhere like that in the south of England, he might have been considered very small beer. Mainwaring liked throwing his weight around and had probably, instead of selling his aunt's house and croft, chosen to stay in this small pond to perform as a big fish.

'I will call on you tomorrow,' said Hamish, 'and tell you how I got on. Address?'

'Balmain. It's about two miles outside the town on the Lochdubh road.'

Hamish wrote it down.

'Goodbye, Constable,' said Mainwaring. 'But you will find the hostility is directed against my wife. She puts people's backs up.'

'I have found,' said Hamish slowly, 'that married people often don't think much of each other. I mean, if the couple is popular, each one takes the credit. If unpopular, each assumes the other is to blame.'

Mainwaring turned in the doorway, his eyes bulging. 'Are you aware of what you have just said?' he shouted. 'You are a cheeky blighter, and if I don't get results from you by tomorrow, then I'll have you out of Cnothan so fast, your feet won't touch the ground!'

'I wass thinking aloud,' said Hamish sadly. 'A bad, bad fault. Now don't fash yourself, sir. Arresting the witches is part of my job.'

The crash of the door as Mainwaring slammed out was his only answer.

'I shouldnae ha' said that,' mourned Hamish, fishing a packet of biscuits out of one of the shopping bags, opening it, and giving one to his dog. 'But of a' the conceited men!'

He helped himself to a biscuit and stared into space. There was something about Mainwaring that didn't ring true. That 'cheeky blighter' was the sort of thing an ex-army man would say in a bad play.

He decided to go out and collect as much gossip about Mainwaring as he could before seeing the minister's wife again.

He made himself dinner, walked Towser, and then set off down the main street, reflecting that there was no point in trying out MacGregor's car until he had farther afield to go.

He went to the churchyard with his torch and poked about. Great Celtic crosses reared up against the night sky. Frost was already glittering on the gravel paths. They were raked smooth and there was not a sign of even one footstep. Deciding to have a word with Mrs Mainwaring the following day and persuade her to come with him and show him exactly where the witches had appeared, Hamish went back to the churchyard gate and let himself out.

Down on the waterfront was a bar called The Clachan. Hamish pushed open the door and went in. It was a dreary smoke-filled room with a juke-box blaring melancholy country-and-western songs from a corner. It was a Monday night and so few of the regulars were in, having spent all their money on the

Saturday. Hamish ordered a bottle of beer and took it over to a table by the window and sat down.

The cowboy on the juke-box, who had been complaining that his son called another man Daddy, wailed off into silence.

The door opened and a tall, slim man walked in. Hamish observed him curiously. He had carefully waved hair, horn-rimmed glasses, a sallow skin, and buck-teeth. He was wearing a city suit of charcoal-grey worsted with a checked shirt, and tight waistcoat under a camel-hair coat.

He ordered a gin and tonic and then turned and faced the room. His eyes fell on Hamish. He hesitated and then walked over. Incomer, thought Hamish. No local would approach a strange policeman. The minister's wife, who felt such gestures to be her duty, did not count.

'You're Macbeth,' he said. 'I'm Harry Mackay.'

'You don't look as if you belong here,' said Hamish.

'Oh, I was brought up here, but I spent a good part of my life in Edinburgh,' said Mackay.

'And what brought you back?'

'I'm an estate agent. I work for Queen and Earl.'

'I didn't pass your office in the main street,' said Hamish.

'No, you wouldn't,' said Mackay. 'Estate agents are regarded with suspicion. My office is on the other side of the loch, among the council houses.'

'You can't do much business in this part of Sutherland,' said Hamish, watching as the estate agent lit a cigarette with a gold Dunhill lighter.

'Oh, it would surprise you, Macbeth. Do you know Baran Castle?'

'Aye, it's that big place over to the west. Bought by an American last year.'

'Well, I sold that,' said Mackay proudly. 'It's not the locals who give me the business, but the foreigners and expatriots. I sold that castle for over a million pounds. And Kringstein, the local big cheese, bought Strachan House and the estates from me as well. So, how's crime getting on in Cnothan?'

'I have the case of witchcraft already,' said Hamish.

'The haunting of the Mainwarings? Some-one wants that pillock out of here and I can't blame them. Stuck-up bastard.'

'He hasn't crossed you, has he?'

'I thought he meant to,' said Mackay with a grin. 'He's bought two more houses and crofts outside town. Why, nobody knows. He uses the crofts, but the houses just stand empty. His own place is decrofted, and he got the land at the other two decrofted as well. That would be about six years ago. I thought he was going to compete with me by putting them on the market, but not him. Crofts are a pain in the neck to an estate agent anyway.'

There was a short silence while both contemplated the peculiarities of crofting. The word 'croft' comes from the Gaelic *coirtean*, meaning a small enclosed field. In early times in the crofting counties of Shetland, Orkney, Caithness, Sutherland, Ross and Cromarty, Inverness, and Argyll, there was a belief that lengthy tenancy gave right to a 'kindness', or permanency of settlement. But the Highland Clearances of the last century, when the crofters were driven off their hill farms to turn Sutherland into one large sheep ranch, had caused bitter hardship. The Crofting Act was passed to ensure security of tenure; this ended landlord absolutism. Once a crofter had tenancy of his croft or hill farm, he could be sure of no interference from the landlord and he no longer had any fear of being driven off. The crofter could also get the land decrofted – that is, buy it from the landowner at a reasonable price – but few crofters did this. Most were fearful of change, preferring to hang on to their small uneconomical croft units and collect the government grants. Sometimes unscrupulous estate agents let their clients who were buying an old croft house as a holiday home believe that the croft land went along with it. This practice left the buyers to find out for themselves that crofting land must be worked all the year round or the tenancy is refused by the Crofters Commission, and the assignation of the croft can be blocked by the neighbours anyway, who put up objections to any incomer simply as a matter of habit.

Hamish broke the silence first. 'Was there no objection to him getting the other two crofts when he had one already?' he asked.

'People didn't dislike him as much then as they do now. The two crofts are adjoining the one he inherited from his aunt. But they're surrounded by moors for miles. There are no other crofters near enough to him to put up a fight. Most of the crofts are to the other side of Cnothan. Besides, it's happening all over. Some of these crofters have enough land to make up a good-sized farm. Of course, unlike Mainwaring, they don't bother decrofting it, for they're afraid of losing the government grants if they do.'

'And no objection from the landowner?'

'Kringstein. Couldn't care less. You know he hardly gets any rents to speak of from the croft land. Besides, the crofter has more power in the matter than the landowner. The landowner's got to sell to the crofter if asked and at a ridiculously low price, too. Mainwaring's not short of a bob, and I could have got the owners of these houses a lot more money. He went along with cash and they sold cheap.

'Speak of the devil,' said Mackay, twisting his head round. 'Here he comes.'

Mainwaring had just entered and walked up to the bar. He was followed by two enormous Sutherland men, both well over six feet in height.

'And who are his companions?' asked Hamish, feeling he should escape before Mainwaring saw him, but being held to his seat by curiosity.

'Alistair Gunn is the one with the leather hat on,' said Mackay. 'He works for the Forestry Commission and makes money on the side by working as a ghillie when the toffs come up from London. His friend, Dougie Macdonald, is a ghillie when he's not collecting his dole and sleeping.'

Hamish had heard that the local landowner, Mr Kringstein, a toilet-roll manufacturer, ran his home and estates in the time-honoured way. Contrary to gloomy expectations, he went on much as the aristocrat he had bought the land and estates from had done. The ghillies, or Highland servants, made their money when Kringstein had a house party. They went out on the river with the guests and showed them, if necessary, how to fish, and carried their tackle and rowed them up and down.

It was obvious to Hamish that the two ghillies wanted to get away from Mainwaring, but were kept by his side because they had accepted his self-appointed role as laird, much as they resented it. 'Do ye know what happened to my aunt the other day?' said Alistair Gunn. 'She was on the bus to Golspie and wearing her new fur coat and she could hear this bairn behind her, chattering to its mither, and then she smelt oranges, and the next thing she knew, she could feel something rubbing at the back of her new fur coat.'

'Oh, for heaven's sake,' said Mainwaring testily, 'that happened to everyone's aunt, and the story is as old as the hills. You were about to say that the next thing your aunt heard was the kid's mother saying, "Don't do that, dear. You'll get fur all over your orange."'

'I wass not about to say that,' said Alistair Gunn. 'Not at all. It was a different thing entirely.'

'Then what was it?' asked Mainwaring, his voice full of amused contempt.

'Well, I am not going to tell you, because you are not going to listen,' said Alistair huffily.

'You mean you can't tell me,' jeered Mainwaring. 'The trouble with you chaps is that you hear an old story or a joke on the radio and immediately you decide it's something funny that happened to your aunt or uncle.'

The pub door opened and two other men came in. Alistair and his friend hailed them with relief.

'Dearie me,' said Hamish. 'Does he always go on like that?'

'Always,' said Mackay gloomily. 'He's spotted you. Here he comes.'

Mackay reflected he had never seen anyone move with such speed. One minute, the constable was sitting at his ease; the next, he had darted out of the door.

Mainwaring dived after him. 'Macbeth!' he called. But there was no movement in the darkness.

Hamish, who had run around the side of the pub, waited a few moments, and then started to walk towards the manse.

But there was no friendly welcome from Mrs Struthers. The minister was there, and so, with many nervous looks at her husband, Mrs Struthers said there was no one at the Women's Rural Institute who would behave in such a way, and no one in Cnothan had any reason to wish the Mainwarings ill.

Hamish went sadly back to the police station. He felt homesick. He did not switch on the lights when he got to the police station, but sat on the floor of the kitchen with the curtains drawn and the little television set on the floor in front of him.

After fifteen minutes, he heard the bell at the police-station end resounding furiously through the house, followed a few minutes later by knocking on the kitchen door.

Towser let out a low growl and Hamish shushed the dog into silence.

After a while, he could hear footsteps crunching away over the gravel, and then there was silence. Mr Mainwaring had gone home.

Hamish switched on the lights, put the television set on the table, and made himself a cup of coffee. A female newscaster with flat, pale eyes was talking about famine in Ethiopia and making Hamish feel he was personally responsible for it. He switched channels. There was a programme about wildlife in the Galapagos Islands. He settled down to watch.

And then there was a knock at the kitchen door again.

He cocked his head to one side and listened. Whoever it was had chosen to come straight to the kitchen door rather than go to the police-station end.

He softly approached the door and listened again. He felt sure if Mainwaring had returned, then he would feel the man's anger through the door.

He suddenly opened it. A couple stood on the step, blinking in the light.

'Constable Macbeth?' said the man. 'I am

John Sinclair, and this is my wife, Mary. We're in need of a bit of help.'

'Come in,' said Hamish, leading the way into the kitchen. He pulled out chairs for them and switched on the electric kettle and took cups and saucers down from the cupboard.

'And what can I do for you, Mr Sinclair?' said Hamish, measuring tea-leaves into the teapot.

'We're friends of Mr Johnson, the hotel manager, over at Lochdubh.'

'Aye, I know him well.'

'He told us you might be able to help us. We wass over in Lochdubh the other day. My brother, Angus, has the fishing boat there.'

'I know Angus. No trouble in Lochdubh, is there?' asked Hamish sharply.

'No, none whateffer,' said John Sinclair. He took off his tweed cap and twisted it round and round in his fingers. His wife, Mary, lit up a cigarette and Hamish sniffed the air longingly. He had given up smoking two months ago and wondered if the sharp desire for nicotine would ever leave him. Priscilla Halburton-Smythe disapproved of smoking.

Hamish filled the teapot with boiling water and tipped some of the biscuits from the packet on the table on to a plate. He sat down beside them, poured tea, cast an anguished look at Mary Sinclair's cigarette, and then said, 'What's it about?'

'It's like this,' said John Sinclair. 'My faither lives outside the town on the road to Lochdubh, not far, about a mile up the road, say. He's got a bit croft and a cottage. My mither died two years ago, and since then Faither's shut himself up. He won't see me or Mary or his wee grandson or anyone.'

'And what is it I can do?' asked Hamish.

'Mr Johnson told us you had the gift o' the gab,' said John Sinclair. 'We wass hoping you could go out and see Faither and have a blether with him, and see if you can cheer him up.'

Hamish began to feel cheered up himself. This was just the sort of family problem he was often asked to deal with in Lochdubh, where the policeman doubled as local psychiatrist.

'I've got business out that way with Mr Mainwaring,' said Hamish. 'I'll drop by to see your father in the morning.'

John Sinclair had a typically Sutherland type of face, high cheek-bones and intense blue eyes that slanted at the corners in an almost oriental way. Those eyes went blank.

'Och, I wouldnae bother yourself with the crabbit auld man,' said Mary Sinclair, speaking for the first time. She was a small, fat woman with dyed blonde hair cut in what Hamish was already beginning to think of as the Cnothan cut, short and chrysanthemum-like, a style which had been fashionable in the fifties. 'Thanks for the tea. We'd best be on our way.'

'I am not a friend of Mr Mainwaring's,' said Hamish, correctly interpreting the reason for the sudden coolness in the air. 'I am investigating the attack on his wife.'

'Attack!' Mary Sinclair looked amazed.

'Three people dressed as witches jumped out at her last night,' said Hamish.

'Oh, that.' Mary shrugged. 'They didnae hurt her, jist gave her the wee fright.'

Hamish looked at her sharply. 'You don't seem very shocked. And anyway, why Mrs Mainwaring? Why not Mr Mainwaring, who seems to be the one nobody likes?'

'I don't know a thing about it,' said Mary quickly, 'but if you ask me, you could poison that man, and he'd still be in Cnothan in the morning. Nothing would get rid of him.'

'And so the vulnerable one is attacked? Nasty,' said Hamish. 'I mean, the weaker one,' he added in reply to Mary's blank look.

'I don't know a thing about it,' she said again. She dragged on her cigarette. Hamish waited for the smoke to appear but it did not. He wondered where it went, or if Mary Sinclair went around with fog-bound lungs.

'Don't be tellin' that Mainwaring any of our business,' said John Sinclair. 'We keep ourselves to ourselves in Cnothan.'

'Aye,' said Hamish dryly. 'I had noticed that. I'll call on your father tomorrow.'

After the Sinclairs had left, Hamish turned back to the television. The wildlife programme had ended and now a couple with almost unintelligible Birmingham accents were writhing on a bed. He wondered why it was that the actresses television chose for the passionate sex scenes were always scrawny, sallow, and angry-looking. He tried the other channels. On one, the news again, on another, an 'alternative' comedian was making up in four-letter words what he lacked in wit, and on the third, there was the umpteenth rerun of *The Quiet Man*. He switched off the set and stared moodily into space. The wind had risen and was tearing through the trees outside the house. He felt lonely and miserable. Then he thought of Jenny Lovelace, and a little glimmer of light appeared on the horizon of his depression.

The morning was glaring bright and freezing cold. He crossed the road and knocked on the door of Jenny's cottage. There was no reply. Feeling cold and miserable again, he returned to the police station and got out MacGregor's white police Land Rover, noticing without much surprise that it was nearly out of petrol.

He stopped at the garage, calling out 'Fine Day' to the petrol pump attendant, who grunted by way of reply and looked at him with hard, hostile eyes.

Hamish waited until the tank was filled up, paid for the petrol, and then said to the petrol-pump attendant, 'That's a nasty, stupid face you've got, you unfriendly, horrible man.'

He drove off, leaving the man staring after him, and headed out on the Lochdubh road, wishing with all his heart he was going home. Just on the outskirts of the town were several long, low, white-washed buildings with a sign outside that read CNOTHAN GAME AND FISH COMPANY.

Hamish decided to call in on the way back and see if he could scrounge anything.

The natives appeared to grow friendlier the farther he drove out of Cnothan. By asking a man on a tractor, he was able to find out that Diarmuid Sinclair, John's father, lived on the hill up on the left of the road a few yards farther on.

There was a path leading up to a small white croft house, but no drive. He parked the Land Rover in the ditch and walked up towards the house.

No smoke came from the chimney and the curtains were tightly drawn. And yet, mused Hamish, the old man could not be too much of a recluse, for the fencing around the croft was in good repair and there was a fair-sized flock of Cheviots cropping the grass.

He knocked on the low door but there was no reply. The wind soughed and whistled through the stunted trees that formed a shelter belt to one side of the house. A flock of sea-gulls wheeled overhead and then landed in the field in front of the house. 'Bad weather coming,' muttered Hamish. He tried the handle of the door and found it unlocked. He opened it and went in.

Like most croft houses, it had a parlour, seldom used, to one side, and a living-room-cum-kitchen on the other. He went into the kitchen.

Diarmuid Sinclair sat beside the cold hearth wrapped in a tartan blanket. He looked like one of the minor prophets or the Ancient Mariner seeking one of three to stoppeth. He had a long white beard and glittering eyes, bushy eyebrows, and a rosy, wrinkled face.

'Blowing up outside,' said Hamish. 'Cold in here. Want the fire lit?'

Diarmuid looked at him with the sorrowful eyes of a whipped dog, but said nothing.

Hamish made a clicking noise of impatience. He went back outside and round the house to the peat stack and collected some peats. He chopped kindling and took the lot back indoors and proceeded to light the fire.

When it was crackling merrily, he swung the smoke-blackened kettle on its chain over the blaze and then went to a shelf in the corner and found mugs, a carton of milk, and a jar of instant coffee. When the kettle was boiling, he made the coffee, put in plenty of sugar, and, fishing in his pocket, produced a flask of whisky and poured a generous measure in one cup.

He handed the cup to the old man, who drew a wrinkled hand out from under his rug and waved it away.

'I am not wasting good whisky,' said Hamish severely. 'Drink it, ye miserable old sinner, or I'll arrest ye for impeding the law in the process of its duty.'

'I am the sick man,' quavered Diarmuid.

'You look it,' said Hamish heartlessly. 'And it's no wonder, sitting there feeling sorry for yourself and too damn lazy to light your own fire.'

Diarmuid drank a large mouthful of hot coffee and whisky.

'I see you haven't heard the news,' he said drearily. 'Ma wife died.'

'That wass two years ago,' said Hamish. 'And life goes on, and the poor woman can't be having much of a time up there what with worrying about you neglecting your grandson and committing suicide. For that's just what you are doing, you auld scunner.'

'I'm a poor auld man,' wailed Diarmuid.

'You're about sixty, although I admit you've done your best to look like eighty. What on

41

earth are you thinking about to turn your own son and grandson from the door?'

'They don't need me. I'm a poor auld –'

'Oh, shut up,' said Hamish morosely. He walked to the window and looked out on the desolate scene. 'Aye, it's blowing hard and the seagulls are in your fields. There'll be snow before long.'

Diarmuid tilted his mug and drained the rest of the scalding contents in one gulp.

Then he threw back the rug and eased himself to his feet, releasing a strong smell of unwashed body. 'That's where you're wrong,' said Diarmuid. He went to a barometer on the wall and tapped it. 'Never wrong,' he said. 'Says "set fair".'

The wind howled and the first drops of sleet struck the panes of the windows. 'It's wrong,' said Hamish. 'Look. Sleet. It'll turn to snow before evening.'

'Nobody'll listen to a poor auld man,' mourned Diarmuid. 'That machine never makes a mistake.'

Hamish seldom lost his temper, but loneliness, worry that Priscilla might even now be in Lochdubh, and fury at the self-pity of Diarmuid boiled up in him. He seized the barometer from the wall, walked to the front door, and threw it out on the grass. 'See for yourself, you stupid barometer,' he howled.

There was a strange rusty sound from behind him. Ashamed of himself, Hamish ran out and retrieved the barometer, scared he had given Diarmuid a heart attack. The crofter's choking and creaking noises were becoming louder by the minute.

'There, there,' said Hamish, quite frightened. 'Me and my damn temper. Sit down, man.' Diarmuid sank back into his armchair by the fire, still choking, grunting, and wheezing.

It was then that Hamish realized the crofter was laughing.

It was an hour before he left Diarmuid. As if the laughter had broken his self-imposed isolation, the crofter would not stop talking. Hamish found the croft house boasted a surprisingly modern bathroom at the back and coaxed Diarmuid to take a bath. Then he fried him eggs and bacon, made him a pot of strong tea laced with more whisky, and went on his way, promising to call again.

As he had forecast, the sleet was already changing to snow as he turned the Land Rover in to the short drive that led to Balmain.

Balmain was a bungalow, and not a very good one either. It was a square, thin-walled affair with a temporary look, having the appearance of some lakeside summerhouses. The original croft house stood close by, now

being used as a shed. Some scraggly welling-
tonias acted as a shelter belt. He rang the doorbell, which sounded like Big Ben, and waited.

He had imagined Mrs Mainwaring would
turn out to be a small, faded, timid woman,
but it was a giantess who answered the door.
Mrs Mainwaring was nearly six feet tall. She
was powerfully built and had an enormous
bust and a great tweed-covered backside,
which she wordlessly displayed to Hamish as
she turned and walked off into the house, leaving the door open. He followed her in and
found himself in a book-lined living-room. A
quick curious glance at the titles told Hamish
that it was doubtful the shelves contained one
work of fiction, either classical or modern.
There were a great number of 'How to' books
on carpentry, painting, sheep-rearing, art, and
gardening. There were shelves of books on
popular psychology, and row upon row of
encyclopaedias and dictionaries. There were
two easy chairs, a low coffee-table, a desk with
a typewriter, two filing cabinets, and a large
Persian rug on the floor. There were no knick-
knacks or ornaments, no magazines or newspapers. And the room was cold. The fireplace
was ugly, being made of acid-green tiles. A
single log smouldered dismally, occasionally
sending puffs of smoke out into the stale, cold
air of the room.

'Sit down, officer,' said Mrs Mainwaring in

a deep voice. 'My husband is out somewhere at the moment. He told me he had been to see you.'

'I wondered,' said Hamish, looking round for a place to lay his cap and finally setting it neatly on the coffee table, 'if you would mind coming with me to the churchyard and showing me exactly where it was you were attacked.'

'I wasn't attacked,' said Mrs Mainwaring. 'Just startled. Not every day I see witches.' She gave a sudden bellowing laugh.

'Whateffer,' said Hamish politely. 'When would it be convenient for you to visit the scene of the crime?'

'It wouldn't be convenient,' said Mrs Mainwaring. 'William would just say I was making a fuss.'

'But your husband is most insistent that I find out who frightened you.'

'He likes poking his nose into things and annoying people,' said Mrs Mainwaring. 'Annoying the replacement constable must be the breath of life to him.'

'Would you say you were unpopular in the community?' asked Hamish.

'*I'm* not. He is,' said Mrs Mainwaring roundly. 'In fact, I like this place. Nice people.'

'I would not say that they are very friendly to incomers, even someone like myself from the west coast,' Hamish pointed out.

'Well, they're not hypocrites like the English,' boomed Mrs Mainwaring, as if speaking of a nationality other than her own. 'They're all right when you get to know them. William got soured, that's all. He ran about at the beginning being charming to everyone and they rebuffed him, and so now he wants his revenge on the lot of them.'

Hamish sighed and took out his notebook. 'Now, Mrs Mainwaring, if we can just get down to the facts.'

'Put your book away. I can't be bothered. I am not really interested in who it is. I can't take something like that personally when it was all directed at William.'

'What shall I tell your husband?'

For the first time a little crack appeared in Mrs Mainwaring's self-assured manner. 'Have a whisky,' she said, and lumbered out of the room without waiting for an answer.

'The coffee will do just fine,' Hamish called after her. 'I am driving.'

There was no reply. She was gone a long time. At last she returned with a whisky decanter, a syphon of soda, and a cup of coffee and a plate of scones.

She put the coffee in front of Hamish and then poured herself an enormous glass of whisky and soda and lit a cigarette. She poured the drink down her throat and let out a long sigh.

There came the sound of a car approaching. Mrs Mainwaring moved like lightning. She stubbed out her cigarette and opened the window, letting the gale howl through the room. She seized the whisky decanter, the ashtray, and her glass and ran out.

In what seemed like two seconds she was back, breathing heavily and smelling strongly of peppermint. She closed the window and sat down primly on the edge of a chair.

Mainwaring came into the room. 'So you've actually turned up,' he said to Hamish. 'Who did it?'

'I don't know,' said Hamish mildly. 'I was just interviewing your wife.'

'You won't get much sense out of Agatha,' said Mainwaring. His small blue eyes turned on his wife. 'What are you wearing that old tweed skirt and jumper for? Didn't that dress I ordered from the mail order arrive yesterday?'

'Yes, dear,' said Mrs Mainwaring meekly. 'I was saving it for best.'

'And what is a better occasion than your husband's company? Go and put it on.'

Mrs Mainwaring's colour was high as she left the room. A moment later there came the sound of a car starting up.

'Gone off in a huff, as usual,' said Mainwaring. 'Now, I assume you have already dusted the churchyard wall for fingerprints.'

'No, I haven't,' said Hamish crossly. 'I suggest the best thing to do is to phone Strathbane and ask them to send a team from Forensic. They won't budge for me but they might do it for you. Not that there'll be any fingerprints worth having from that wall, and since it was probably not done by hardened criminals, even if you got fingerprints, it wouldn't do much good.'

'What you are trying to say is that you're damned lazy and don't want to be bothered,' said Mainwaring.

Hamish got to his feet. 'I will investigate the case for you as I would for anyone, but I would get further and faster without the hindrance of your insulting and spiteful remarks. You've got a nasty tongue. I want a quiet time here and I don't want another murder investigation. So if you want my advice, stop putting people's backs up or you'll end up at the bottom of Loch Cnothan one of these days!'

Chapter Three

How beastly the bourgeois is
especially the male of the species –
– D. H. Lawrence

Bewildered and unhappy, Hamish drove off. He had lost his temper two times that morning when he normally lost it only about two times a year. Far away, at the foot of the long, twisting road, he could see the houses of Cnothan. From this distance, the town had a temporary look, as if this ancient land of rock and thin earth was one day going to give a massive shrug and send all these petty humans and their squabbles to eternity. It was as if the land itself did not like incomers, or, as they were often jeeringly called in the Highlands, white settlers. An ancient hostility emanated from the fields, from the humped Neolithic ruins that dotted the landscape.

Across the fields came the dreary *om-pom* of a diesel train's klaxon, tugging at something in

49

Hamish's memory. The sound of a diesel train, he thought, was never so haunting as the whistle of the old steam trains, which could conjure up visions of bleak distances with one solitary wail.

He slowed as he came to the Cnothan Game and Fish Company. There was something so cheerful and friendly and prosperous about the place that Hamish drove in and sauntered toward the office.

A very small, gypsy-looking man came out to meet him. 'Jamie Ross,' he said, holding out his hand. 'You're just in time for coffee.'

'I'm Hamish Macbeth.'

'I know,' said Jamie. 'Who doesn't? Sit yourself down.'

There was a jug of steaming coffee standing ready, made by one of those American coffee machines that first pioneered good coffee in the Highlands of Scotland, replacing the bitter sludge which had masqueraded as coffee before.

The office was bright and warm. 'Do a lot of business?' asked Hamish.

'Aye, but mostly with London. Lobsters, smoked salmon, and venison. I've just bought three new refrigerated trucks to take the goods down to the market at Billingsgate. Finish your coffee and I'll give you a tour.'

While Hamish drank his coffee, Jamie continued to talk proudly of his business, how he had four fishing boats over on the west coast and was well on the way to making himself a fortune.

Then he took Hamish round the long, low buildings. One housed deer carcasses, giant beasts pathetic in death, row upon row of them. The next building was a shop that sold commercial frozen packaged meals as well as smoked salmon, pheasant, grouse, and partridge. The last building they came to had three enormous lobster tanks, each surrounded by a low concrete wall, the water alive with crawling black lobsters. 'See this one,' said Jamie, lifting a black monster out of the water. 'Eight pounds in weight.'

'And how much will that fetch in London?' asked Hamish.

'Oh, about twenty-five pounds. In fact, you could say about a pound sterling for every year of its life. That lobster's about twenty-five years old.'

'So how much is in the three tanks – I mean, how much is all this worth?'

Jamie grinned. 'There's about six thousand pounds' worth in each tank. The water's salt, of course, and the filters you hear bubbling away there keep the water clean.'

'Man, you must be kept busy,' marvelled Hamish. 'Ever get a day off?'

'Haven't had one in years,' said Jamie. 'But I'll be going down to Inverness at the weekend for my son's wedding. All the family'll be there, so I'll need someone to mind the store for the first time.'

'Would you like me to drop in at the week-end and see if everything's all right?' volunteered Hamish.

'No, nothing can go wrong. I'm not worried about burglars. Never had a break-in in Cnothan. I'm more worried about the filters packing up. I've got a local man, Sandy Carmichael, who's going to act as watchman.'

Hamish raised his eyebrows. 'Not the town drunk, him with the horrors.'

'The same. But he's going straight and there's no harm in him at all. Of course, Mainwaring got to hear of it and dropped by to warn me and yak on about how dangerous it was to employ a drunk. I hate that man; I'd feed him to the fish if I thought I'd get away with it. Interfering, pontificating nuisance. I liked him at first. Funny, that. He was a breath of fresh air. Charming, friendly. Then he buys a book on scientific fish-farming and tries to involve me in it. No business head whatsoever. Or I assume the man has no business head, for I was to put up the money for the venture, which he would run. I fended him off as politely as I could. He became more insistent. Then he started to get rude and make some patronizing remarks about how ill-run my business was. I wanted to buy one of those croft houses out beyond his for my uncle. I told him about it when we were friends. Next thing I know, he's bought the place himself, and now it stands empty. I know he did it to spite me. I was not interested in the land, only in the house for my uncle. Mainwaring uses the croft land, of course, or the Crofters Commission would step in.'

'Why?' asked Hamish. 'I mean, why does he put people's backs up?'

'I think he likes power,' said Jamie, 'and irritating people is a sort of twisted way of getting it. See here, I can't believe my luck. I've worked hard, but I was a road worker's boy and came up from nothing. At the back of my mind, there's always the fear that all this will melt away like the fairy gold. Mainwaring senses that and does his best to make me feel insecure. He'd make a good blackmailer.'

'Would you say his wife is frightened of him?' asked Hamish, enjoying all this gossip immensely.

'Aye, and I wonder why. She's a big, strong woman, and though he's a big, strong man, you'd think she could still make mincemeat of him if she liked. You know that business o' the witches?'

Hamish nodded.

'Well, I wouldn't put it past him to have stage-managed the whole thing himself. Mrs Mainwaring likes a dram, and she was a bit squiffy yesterday morning and told Mrs Grant in the town that she thought he was jealous of her popularity. Mrs Grant told Mrs MacNeill, who told Mrs Struthers, who told my wife, who told me.'

'Some marriages are awf'y sad,' said Hamish.

'They are that,' agreed Jamie, 'and none so sad as the Mainwarings'.'

Hamish thought deeply for a few moments, and then said, 'I am still surprised he got the extra croft land just like that. There's a lot of land greed in the Highlands.'

'Like I said, he was popular in the beginning,' said Jamie, 'although I don't believe the man knew it. He took shyness and diffidence among the locals for rebuff. Then his aunt had been very well-liked in the community. They didn't like to put up objections. When they did, it was too late. You know crofters, Hamish. They don't know their own laws. They learn distorted facts from each other by word of mouth. It was just after he acquired the crofts that he started throwing his weight about.'

'So his aunt wasn't English?'

'Oh, no. But as far as I can gather, Mainwaring was born and brought up in England. His aunt, Mrs Drummond, had been here since the day of her marriage about fifty years ago. Brian Drummond, her husband, died about ten years before she did. I think the Mainwarings are quite rich and Mrs Drummond belonged to the mother's side, which hadn't much of the ready. Mainwaring came up on a lot of flying visits before she died.'

'And who was it objected to him getting the crofts?'

'Two of them. Alec Birrell over at Dunain, that's on the other side of Cnothan, and Davey Macdonald, also from Dunain. How Mainwaring got to learn who had written in to object to him, I'm not sure, except at that time he was friendly with that wee weasel who works at the Crofters Commission, Peter Watson, so he could've told him. Anyway, a few months after they objected, both lost a couple of dozen sheep each one night. They accused Mainwaring of having taken them away out of spite, but since there was no proof and the sheep were never found, there was nothing Sergeant MacGregor could do.'

Heartened by the friendly visit, Hamish returned to the police station. He saw, as he drove past, that Jenny was working in her gallery. Once inside the station, he brushed his hair and his uniform. The snow was still blowing past the window, but it was getting thinner and tinged with pale yellow as the sun fought to get through. He picked a bottle of aftershave out of the bathroom cabinet. MacGregor's. It was called Muscle, and the advertising on the packet said it was for truly masculine men. Hamish opened it and sniffed. It smelled pleasantly of sandalwood. He splashed some on his chin, and feeling quite strange and exotic, for he had never used after-shave before, he decided to go across the road and visit Jenny Lovelace.

And then the phone in the office began to ring. Cursing, he went through to answer it.

The voice at the other end was husky and Highland. 'Murder,' it said. 'A body on the top o' Clachan Mohr. Come quick.' And then the receiver at the other end was replaced.

Heart beating hard, Hamish studied the ordnance survey map on the wall. Clachan Mohr was a craggy cliff outside the village, a relic of the ancient days when the long arms of the sea reached into the heart of Sutherland.

He drove at breakneck speed down the main street with the police siren blaring. A mile to the east, dimly visible through the snow, rose the steep sides of Clachan Mohr. He hurtled round the hairpin bends towards it, tyres screeching through the snow, until he parked the Land Rover in its shadows. There was a thin rabbit track of a path winding upwards. He set off, wishing he had worn his climbing boots, for the grass was slippery with snow and he kept sliding back. He was agile and athletic, but it took him nearly half an hour to reach the top. The snow thinned again, and there, at the very edge of the cliff, lay the body of a man, his red pullover clearly distinguishable against the blinding white of the snow. Someone's got Mainwaring, thought Hamish, his mind working out times. How on earth could someone have had time to murder the man on the top of Clachan Mohr when Hamish had seen him only a short time ago?

And then he stiffened when he was still a few yards from the body. All at once, he knew he was being watched. He felt it. Then he thought ... the body is just now getting covered with snow and yet that phone call was *almost an hour ago*.

He stood still, listening with his sixth sense, feeling for where those watchers might be. He sniffed the air like a dog. There was a faint tang of human sweat and stale tobacco. He saw a patch of gorse bushes to his left and suddenly dived towards it. Alistair Gunn and Dougie Macdonald rose sheepishly to their feet. 'I'll deal with you in a minute,' snapped Hamish. He ran to the body. It was, as he had already suspected, a dummy made out of old clothes stuffed with newspapers.

He came back and looked coldly at the two shuffling and grinning ghillies. 'Jist our joke,' said Alistair Gunn.

He had a broad leering grin on his turnip face. Hamish took out his handcuffs and handcuffed the two men together.

'Start walking,' he snapped.

'Cannae ye take a joke?' whined Dougie.

'Shut up!' said Hamish.

The ghillies led the way down, not, to Hamish's high irritation, by the difficult path he had scaled, but by a broad, easy, winding path down the back. He shoved both men into the police Land Rover and drove off, staring angrily through the windscreen. On the edge of Loch Cnothan was a small jetty. Hamish removed the handcuffs from the two men after he had stopped by the jetty. 'Now walk to the end,' he said, 'and keep your backs to me. I don't want to see your stupid faces when I talk to ye.'

'Whit'll happen to us?' moaned Dougie to Alistair.

'Naethin,' said Alistair with a shrug. 'The man's a poofter. Cannae ye smell him?'

This was said in a low voice, but Hamish heard it. It was all he needed. He waited until they were standing facing the water and then he kicked out with all his might, straight at Alistair's broad backside. Alistair went flying into the icy water. 'Dinnae touch me,' screeched Dougie, turning around. 'It wasnae me. It wass him!' Hamish contemptuously pushed him in the chest and he went flying as well.

Hamish stood with his hands on his hips

until he was sure both were able to make it to the shore. Then he climbed in to the Land Rover and drove back to the police station. The snow was turning to rain and his wheels skidded on great piles of slush.

When he reached the station, he changed out of his uniform and put on trousers and a flannel checked shirt. He pulled on his spare navy-blue police sweater over it, and then went over to Jenny's cottage and knocked on the door. There was no reply.

'Damn and blast!' yelled Hamish.

The door suddenly opened and Jenny Lovelace stood there, her hair dripping wet and with a large bath towel wrapped round her. 'I was in the bath,' she said. 'What's the matter? You look desperate.'

Hamish shuffled his boots and a slow blush crept up his thin cheeks. His long lashes dropped quickly to veil his eyes.

'Come in then,' said Jenny when he did not speak. 'I'll put some clothes on.'

While she was getting ready, Hamish took a look at the pictures in the gallery. They were of the Sutherland countryside, but they were pretty – pretty, like the kind of pictures you used to see on old-fashioned calendars. They had not captured the wild, stark, highly individual beauty of Sutherland, and were strangely lifeless and dead. They were competently drawn and the draughtsmanship was excellent. He was examining a view of a path winding through graceful birch trees into a romantic sunset when Jenny came in.

She was wearing faded jeans and a man's checked shirt, much like his own. Her curls were damp and tousled and her feet bare. When she came to stand beside him, she barely reached his shoulder. 'What do you think?' she asked.

'Very good,' said Hamish politely.

'I do quite well with the tourists in the summer. Of course, I charge very low prices. I don't need much. Come through to the kitchen and have some coffee.'

Hamish loped after her. The kitchen was warm and cluttered. A primrose-yellow Raeburn cooker stood against the wall and the table was covered with paints and brushes.

She poured him a cup of coffee and sat opposite him, clearing a space on the table in front of her by sweeping an assortment of stuff to the side with one small dimpled hand, like a child's.

She gave him a gamine grin. 'You're looking better now,' she said. 'I thought the Hound of Heaven was after you.'

'It's this place,' said Hamish ruefully. 'It's getting me down.' He told her about the witchcraft investigation, and then about the fake murder.

'They do have a rather childish sense of fun,' said Jenny defensively.

'Now me myself,' said Hamish, 'I would call it pure and simple malice.'

'Maybe it's because you don't understand the Highlander.'

'I'm one myself.'

'Of course you are,' giggled Jenny. 'Silly of me. You mustn't listen to all this rubbish about poor Agatha Mainwaring. She's one of those women who deliberately goads her husband into being nasty so that she can play the martyr.'

'That's one way o' looking at it,' said Hamish slowly.

'Never mind the Mainwarings,' said Jenny. 'Tell me about yourself. Married?'

'No. Are you?'

'I was. In Canada. It didn't work out. He was jealous of my painting. He was an artist himself. At my first exhibition in Montreal, he waited until one minute before the show opened and then told me he had always thought my work was too chocolate-box and I wasn't to be disappointed if the critics panned it. I never forgave him.'

Hamish looked at her curiously. 'I would never have guessed ye to be one of those Never-Forgive sort of people. Every husband or wife usually says something crashingly tactless they wouldn't dream of saying to a friend.'

'But not about my painting,' said Jenny fiercely. 'I put my whole personality into my work. He was insulting me and everything I stood for. Can't you see that?'

'Yes, yes,' said Hamish soothingly, although one hazel eye slid to an oil painting on the kitchen wall. It was of a Highland cottage situated on a heathery hill: competent, colourful, and yet lifeless.

'Anyway,' said Jenny, 'we're talking about me and I meant to find out about you.'

Hamish settled back and began to describe his life in Lochdubh and told several very tall and very Highland stories that set Jenny giggling.

'And what about your love life?' she suddenly asked.

'Is there any more coffee?' Hamish held out his cup.

'Meaning you won't talk about it.' Jenny laughed. She went over to the Raeburn, where a glass coffee-pot had been placed to keep warm. Hamish eyed her appreciatively. She was everything Priscilla was not. Jenny was small and plumpish in all the right places, with that tousled hair. Priscilla was never tousled, always cool, slim, blonde, and efficient. Priscilla would never have a cluttered kitchen like this. And Priscilla would never spill hot coffee on her bare feet as Jenny had just done, for Priscilla never spilt anything and Priscilla would never go around on her bare feet. In fact, thought Hamish, feeling more cheerful than he had done in a long time, Priscilla is a pill.

They chatted for some time until Hamish reluctantly said he'd better get back to the police station.

'Come any time,' said Jenny.

'I will,' said Hamish Macbeth. She held out her hand and he took it in his. The physical reaction of his own body amazed him. He looked down at her in surprise, holding her hand tightly.

'Goodbye,' said Jenny, tugging her hand free.

The snow had melted and great sheets of rain were whipping through the town, Hamish noticed in a bemused way. Towser watched him reproachfully as he entered. Hamish donned his waterproof cape and put the dog on the lead and went out to the shops.

The butcher's shop was a cheery, gossipy oasis in the desolation of Cnothan. The butcher, John Wilson, had heard all about the ducking of the ghillies and wanted the details firsthand. Hamish gossiped happily and came away with a bonus of two free lamb chops and a bag of bones for Towser.

He went into the grocer's next door and bought a bottle of wine, vaguely planning to ask Jenny to dinner as soon as possible. He then went into the hardware, which was farther up the street, to buy a corkscrew. He thought there might be one in the bar but did not want to poke around that horrible lounge of the MacGregors to look for it. 'Get it yourself,' said the owner of the shop. 'It's over there on the left.' The accent was English but the manner was pure Cnothan. Hamish wondered if the outsiders became as rude as the locals in sheer self-defence.

In the Clachan, Alistair Gunn and Dougie Macdonald were suffering the taunts of William Mainwaring. 'So your joke backfired,' jeered Mainwaring, 'and the pair of you let that copper shove you in the loch.'

'Weel, ye haff to go carefully when you're dealing with a poofter,' growled Alistair Gunn.

'What are you talking about?' demanded Mainwaring.

'He means Macbeth,' said Dougie in his high sing-song Highland whine. 'The man is a fairy, a homosexual. You should have smelt him. He wass stinking of the perfume.'

Mainwaring looked amazed. 'Aye,' said Alistair, enjoying startling the Englishman. 'He's wan o' them. I can always tell.'

Mainwaring suddenly burst out laughing and slapped Alistair on the back. 'Well, old chap,' he said, 'it takes one to know one.' And, still laughing, he went off.

Alistair stood there stupidly, mulling over that 'it takes one to know one'. Then a slow feeling of outrage started somewhere in the pit of his stomach and spread throughout his whole body.

'I'll kill that man,' he howled.

Later that evening, Mrs Struthers, the minister's wife, was just finishing a lecture on microwave cooking to the Mothers' Meeting in the church hall. The dishes she had prepared were proudly laid out on a table in front of her. William Mainwaring walked in, his eyes roving about the room, obviously looking for his wife. Mrs Struthers was glad Agatha had not put in an appearance and prayed that Mr Mainwaring would leave as soon as possible.

'And that concludes my lecture,' she said. 'I now have some paper plates and knives and forks here and I would like you ladies to sample my cooking.'

Her mouth gave a nervous twitch as Mainwaring approached the table. 'What a strange selection,' he said in a wondering voice. 'What's that cup of goo?'

'It's a sweet-and-sour sauce,' said Mrs Struthers.

'And what's it made of?'

'Pineapple juice and marmalade and a spoonful of vinegar.'

'Yech!' said Mainwaring. 'And look at that baked potato. It doesn't look cooked.'

He seized a fork. Mrs Struthers made a sort of dismal bleating sound like a lamb lost on a dark hillside. She knew that potato hadn't been in long enough, and she had been hoping to slide it away to the side.

'Hard as hell,' cried Mainwaring triumphantly. 'Look, if you want to know about microwave cookery, it's all very simple.' He moved round the table and began a lecture. Woman eyed each other uneasily, and then, with that peculiar Highland talent for disappearing from an awkward situation, the audience gradually melted away.

Mrs Struthers fought back tears as she looked at her cooking. There were some splendid dishes there. 'I'd better be off, then,' said Mainwaring, abruptly cutting short his lecture when he realized he was addressing an empty room.

When the door had closed behind him, Mrs Struthers sat down and began to cry. She picked up a bottle of British sherry she had used for cooking and took a gulp from it. For the first time in her blameless life, she knew what it was to want to kill someone.

* * *

Mainwaring returned to The Clachan. When he had finished tormenting someone, he immediately had to find another victim. His eyes fell on Harry Mackay, sitting over in a corner. He went to join him.

'Business must be bad these days,' said Mainwaring cheerfully.

'What makes you say that?' asked Harry Mackay sourly.

'Just that no one seems to want property these days and you spend most of your time in here.'

'Like yourself,' said the estate agent nastily.

'I wonder what your employers in Edinburgh would think if they knew exactly how little work you do,' said Mainwaring.

'You wouldn't . . .' gasped Harry Mackay.

'I just might,' laughed Mainwaring. 'You know me.'

'Oh, I know you, all right,' said the estate agent bitterly. 'We all know you.'

William Mainwaring at last returned home to see if he could rile his wife to round off the evening. She always claimed she never drank. He searched and searched for the empty bottle but could not find it because Agatha had buried it in the garden. It had been a whole bottle of the cheapest wine possible, called Dream of the Highlands, made by a local winery. She could not risk anything more expensive out of the housekeeping money. She had claimed Hamish had drunk a lot of whisky to explain the low level in the decanter earlier in the day, but there had been no further callers she could use as an excuse and so she had been driven to buy the bottle of cheap wine.

For once, she was armoured against her husband's gibes. Full of Dream of the Highlands, and lost in a rosy fantasy, she barely heard him. She had read an article in the newspapers about the poisoning of an Iraqi businessman in London using a slow-acting rat poison containing thallium, banned in Britain, but available on the Continent. It had a delayed effect and only started to work a week after it was administered. She imagined manufacturing an excuse to visit her sister in Kent. Instead, she would go to Paris and buy the rat poison. Then she would return to Cnothan and poison her husband and promptly set off again, so that when he died, she would be far away from the scene of the crime. A local bobby would not suspect anything. She would start to tell everyone that William had a bad heart.

And so Agatha Mainwaring, with a half-smile on her face, dreamt on, while her husband's voice buzzed and hammered like a wasp against the glass protection of her fantasy.

* * *

'Now, promise me you won't take a dram,' said Jamie Ross, after showing Sandy Carmichael round the premises.

Sandy shuddered. 'I'll neffer touch the stuff again.'

Jamie looked at him uneasily. It would just be like Sandy to go and get drunk and prove Mainwaring right. But Jamie was soft-hearted and knew Sandy needed some money badly, and more than money, he needed the self-respect of being trusted with a job.

Sandy was a tall, thin man in his forties. His face had an unhealthy, bleached look about it, but the hands now holding one of Jamie's coffee-cups were steady. Jamie remembered having to hold Sandy's hands so he could get the coffee down him.

Nothing could really go wrong, Jamie reassured himself. There had never been a burglary in Cnothan. No one even bothered to lock his car.

He wondered whether to ask that policeman to drop in over the weekend just to see that things were all right. But that would show a lack of trust in Sandy, and Sandy certainly did look on the road to recovery.

Hamish found himself surprisingly busy. A sharp phone call from police headquarters to Strathbane told him what MacGregor had not – that he had to patrol a much wider area of surrounding countryside than he had expected. He still found time to call on Diarmuid Sinclair and persuade the crofter to see his family. But to his disappointment, there were no more relaxed coffee sessions with Jenny, who was either painting furiously or not at home. She'd said she went walking to clear her brain. Hamish had offered to go with her, but she said she liked to be alone. Once more, his three months stay in Cnothan stretched out into an eternity of winter days.

Chapter Four

Ah! Who has seen the mailed lobster rise.
– John Hookham Frere

Sandy Carmichael arrived at the Cnothan Game and Fish Company late on Saturday afternoon. Rain had fallen earlier in the day and had now frozen, and the wheels of his old Land Rover crunched over the ice in the yard. Jamie had given him a spare key to the office, where the keys to the sheds hung on a board on the wall.

The office was warm and quiet. Sandy pulled a tattered romance, *The Laird's Passion*, from his pocket, and began to read. Unfortunately, it turned out the laird was a bit of a rake, ripe for reform by the heroine, and in the initial pages, he drank large quantities. Sandy put down the book and stared into space. He hadn't really thought about drinking this past week, the memory of his last bout of the horrors being still fresh in his mind. But now

71

whisky seemed like a golden friend he had harshly misjudged. He could feel the taste of it on his tongue and the warmth of it coiling around his stomach.

He began to fidget, picking up pencils and putting them down. He thought about his last binge. How ill he had been! But he had bought that fish supper from the fish-and-chip shop and some said Murray's fish and chips were cooked in old grease. Maybe it had been food poisoning. Maybe it had been something he had eaten. Or just maybe he was allergic to whisky and he should try drinking wine. Jamie had paid him his wages in advance and the money was there in his pocket, and in Sandy's mind, money and whisky went together.

But he was proud of the fact that Jamie had trusted him and he would not let Jamie down. He would go and patrol the sheds, just like a real watchman.

How eerie the sheds were at night. The fluorescent light still left the corners in darkness. The deer carcasses hung motionless and sad. He moved on to the lobster shed. The water gurgled monotonously in the three tanks.

And then, there, right on the edge of the centre tank, he saw it. A full glass of whisky.

He stared at it, wondering if he were hallucinating. He advanced cautiously, picked it up, and sniffed it. Malt whisky! And, by the smell of it, one of the best malts.

Well, it was only one drink, he reasoned, and stuck out here, he couldn't get any more. One drink never did anyone any harm.

He picked up the glass and took a sip. He took another, larger, sip and the tension of the past week began to leave his body. He'd soon finished the glassful. He felt happy and warm and confident. A few more wouldn't matter. It was Saturday night. The Clachan would be warm and full of company and noise. And he had money.

He would lock up the office, but there was no need to lock the sheds. Jamie never locked them; he was more worried about his filters packing up than he was about crime. Half an hour at The Clachan and then he would come back and settle down and read that romance. A gust of wind howled around the buildings like a banshee. He thought briefly of the haunting of the Mainwarings. That new copper had been questioning an awful lot of people in that innocent-seeming, I-have-just-dropped-by-for-a-gossip way of his. But whoever had frightened Mrs Mainwaring, it hadn't been criminals. The Mainwarings deserved to be driven out of Cnothan – well, him, anyway.

Feeling better than he had in a long time, Sandy drove carefully down into Cnothan. He decided that if Hamish Macbeth was in the bar, then he would buy a packet of cigarettes and take himself off. It was still early evening. There were only a few youths in the bar, all looking remarkably Dickensian in their skin-tight trousers and short jackets. They had pinched white faces and lank hair. Most of them were drunk already, and the giant of a barman, Hector Dunn, was wondering whether that new policeman knew it was part of his duties to turn up at The Clachan on Saturday nights and remove the car keys of anyone who had drunk over the limit.

He tried phoning the police station, but there was no reply. He phoned Jenny Lovelace in case Hamish was there, the gossip about Hamish's visit and attempted visits having spread around the town like wildfire, but she said she hadn't seen him. Her voice sounded funny, as if she were crying.

Hamish was, at that very moment, speeding fast out of Cnothan. A report of an assault on one of the customers at a fishing hotel some thirty miles out of town had just come in.

Sandy drank up a double whisky and ordered another. He immediately became sentimental. When Hector asked him why he wasn't 'minding the store', Sandy said that Jamie Ross knew nothing would happen, and hadn't Jamie in the kindness of his heart left a glass of good whisky on the edge of one of the tanks in the lobster shed for Sandy? It all went to show Jamie knew he, Sandy, could handle his liquor. He put some of his change in the jukebox and selected a Frank Sinatra record and sat down. 'I did it my way,' sang the famous voice. How wise, thought Sandy, nodding his head up and down. Story of my life, he thought. He began to sing along with the record. The youths jeered and catcalled and Hector threw them out.

The bar began to fill up with the locals, men at first, and then later their wives, come to curb the expense of a Saturday night's drinking.

Faces swam in front of Sandy, and voices offered to buy him a drink. The locals were violently jealous of Jamie Ross. Not only did he make a great deal of money, but he did not hide the fact. His new white Mercedes had caused a great deal of heart-burning. To a number of the locals, it seemed like a good joke to get Sandy drunk. Nothing would happen to Jamie's business, of course, but he would be furious when he got back to find his watchman away sleeping off another drinking bout.

Sandy became dimly aware that Hector was demanding his car keys, and with the cunning of the drunk, he said he had walked and did not have his Land Rover with him.

Then Hector was calling 'Time!' and Sandy was aware of the sharp cold outside the pub, of people laughing and teasing him.

He climbed into his rusty Land Rover and then his mind went blank. He drove home in a total drunken blackout.

Sandy Carmichael awoke at noon the following day. His mouth felt like the bottom of a parrot's cage. He drank great gulps of cold water and splashed his face. It was then he remembered his job.

He was still wearing the clothes he had worn the night before. He scrambled out and drove to the Cnothan Game and Fish Company.

His mind worked feverishly, Jamie and his family would be back on the last train. He must get the second half of his wages from Jamie, before Jamie learned, as he surely would, that he had been drinking in The Clachan on Saturday night.

He unlocked the office and then began to calm down. Of course, everything was just as he had left it. He went over to the lobster shed and looked around. The whisky glass was still there. He slipped it into his pocket. He sat down on the edge of the main tank and sighed with relief.

Then he blinked. The water seemed to have a strange pinkish tinge. He slowly scooped a handful of water into the palm of his hand.

Pink.

Then, as he stared at the tank, a piece of torn and shredded jacket slowly rose to the surface and turned over and over in the bubbling water.

He got to his feet and looked down into the lobster tank.

There, underneath the busy, crawling black lobsters, lay a white skeleton, grinning up at him.

Sandy fainted dead away with shock.

When he came round, he staggered up, gloomily deciding he had had a bout of the horrors. But another look into the depths of the pool showed him the skeleton was still there.

Sandy sat down on the edge of the pool. Now fear and shock were sharpening his wits. He thought about that glass of whisky. Jamie couldn't have left it. Some friend of Jamie's must have been sitting in the shed drinking, got drunk, and fallen into the pool and had his body picked clean by the voracious lobsters. But if he called Macbeth, Macbeth would call in a forensic team, and all the lobsters would be taken away along with the skeleton. The whole shed would be sealed off. Eighteen thousand pounds' worth of lobsters! Sandy began to cry. You couldn't insure lobsters, could you? No one would ever trust him again. Jamie wouldn't pay him the second half of his wages and so he would not be able to get a drink to blot out this nightmare. He scrubbed his eyes with his dirty sleeve.

The self-pity of the habitual drunk gripped him. Life was always playing him dirty tricks. Well, he, Sandy, was going to fight back!

He saw a long pole with a net standing in the corner and carefully began to scoop out every bit of clothing. He found a garbage bag and put each shredded piece into it. With his whole body screaming for a drink, he began to search the water to make sure nothing was left. Gold glittered faintly in the light. With mad patience, he fished out the object. It was a gold watch with a few shreds of leather strap still attached to it. He took a deep breath and searched again, poking and moving the crawling black lobsters to see if there was anything left underneath. His search was rewarded. He brought up remains of a leather wallet and scraps of plastic credit cards and pound notes. After that, he found some silver and pennies, which he retrieved by donning a thick pair of work gloves. Shaking and exhausted, he had just decided that must be all when his eyes caught the shine of gold again. Swearing horribly, he resumed his macabre fishing and at last brought up a gold pen. He looked at it curiously, wondering where he had seen it before, and then slipped it into his pocket. A last frantic hunt revealed a pair of false teeth. Shivering and sick, Sandy put them in his pocket as well. Then he eased the net under the skeleton and raised it to the surface. He seized one arm bone and pulled it out. There was a black monster of a lobster clinging to the skeleton and he screamed and tore it off and threw it back in the pool.

His brain had become sharp and clear. The water filters would soon turn the water clear again. The work gloves were nearly in tatters from the claws of the lobsters, so instead of putting them back on the edge of the sink in the corner where he had found them, he added them to the wet and ragged clothes in the bag. He went out and got his Land Rover and backed it up to the shed. He put the bag of clothes and the skeleton in the back and threw an old travelling rug over them.

As he drove off, he could feel the weight of those terrible false teeth dragging at his pocket. He stopped at a bend in the road and hurled the things out of the window, as far away into the gorse and heather as he could manage.

Then he drove to his home, which was a tumbledown cottage outside Cnothan. He took the bag of clothes round the back of his cottage and dumped it down. He siphoned some petrol out of his Land Rover and poured it over the bag and set fire to it. He raked the blaze, turning it over and over, until he was sure all the clothes had been reduced to ash. Then he raked up the ashes and put them in a bag.

He went into his cottage and made himself a cup of hot sweet tea. He took out the watch and pen and laid them on the table. He remembered seeing that pen before.

He longed for a drink so much that his whole body ached and his hands trembled. But he had not finished yet. He remembered the haunting of the Mainwarings and the stories about witchcraft that had buzzed around the town. He drove off again, up out on to the moors. Up against the failing light of the winter sky stood a ring of standing stones, a miniature Stonehenge.

He drove off the road and over the moor towards it, the Land Rover lurching and bumping over the springy turf. He carried the skeleton in his arms into the middle of the standing stones. A ray of setting sun burst through the clouds and shone on to a raised piece of turf in the centre. Sandy gently laid the skeleton down.

It was then he realized that the skull was nearly coming away from the body of the skeleton. He examined it with delicate probing fingers and then let out his breath in a long hiss.

This had been no accident. This was murder.

'If I report this now,' said Sandy aloud, 'they will probably be after me for the murder. If I keep my mouth shut, there'll be money in it for me.'

The sun disappeared and the wind began to howl, tugging at his clothes, as if the spirits of the dead had risen from the moors and were trying to hold him back.

He gave a whimper of fright and began to run.

That evening, Hamish Macbeth saw the light in Jenny's cottage. He was longing for a sympathetic ear. He had gone all the way to the Angler's Rest to find the report of an assault on one of the customers had been false. 'Probably some of the locals playing a joke on you,' the manager had said.

Hamish had stayed to talk, and by the time he had returned to Cnothan, The Clachan was closed. The next day, he had put off trying to see Jenny, but a morning listening to Mr Struthers' sermon and an afternoon interviewing secretive locals about the frightening of Mrs Mainwaring had irritated him immensely.

He saw Jenny moving about and went and knocked on the door. At last she opened it. 'Come in,' she said. Hamish followed her through to her kitchen. 'Will you have a drink?' she asked, turning around.

'What on earth has happened to you, lassie!' cried Hamish, for Jenny's eyes were red with weeping and her face was bloated.

She averted her face. 'I had news of my sister's death,' she said. 'In Canada.'

'I never heard a thing about it,' said Hamish, his mind racing. Relatives, however far away, always phoned the local police station.

'I had a letter,' said Jenny drearily. 'It came yesterday.'

'I am verra sorry,' said Hamish awkwardly. 'Is there anything I can do?'

'Just talk to me.'

'I think it's yourself that needs to do the talking,' said Hamish.

Jenny gave a weak smile. 'I'm being silly,' she said. 'I never liked my sister. We're not very much alike. It was the shock, that's all.'

'And will you be going to Canada for the funeral?'

'No point.' Jenny shrugged. 'We're not a close family.'

'What did she die of?'

'Look, Hamish Macbeth, it's over and done with. I don't want to talk about it. Now, have a drink and tell me about your witch-hunt.'

She produced a bottle of Barsac, a sweet dessert wine, from the fridge, opened it, and poured it into two water glasses.

'Do you often drink this stuff?' asked Hamish, wrinkling his nose.

'What's up with it? It's a drink, isn't it? I forget when I bought it. Oh, I remember. It was last year. It was for some recipe. It's been in the fridge ever since.'

A fat tear rolled down her cheek and splashed into her glass.

Hamish decided to do what he'd been told and chattered on nervously about the fake assault, about how Diarmuid Sinclair was slowly coming out of his shell, about the difficulty of getting any information at all out of the locals.

She drank and listened and seemed soothed. Hamish finally felt he could not talk any longer. He got to his feet. 'I'll be off to my bed, Jenny,' he said. 'Maybe I'll drop by tomorrow, if it is all right with you.'

'Sure. I'll be here.' She came round the kitchen table and stood in front of him, her head bent. 'You don't need to go,' she said.

'*Whit?*'

'Stay the night . . . with me,' said Jenny.

Hamish bent and kissed her cheek. 'It wouldna' work,' he said softly. 'Not when you're this miserable. I'd be someone tae cling to the night, and someone to hate in the morning.'

Jenny remained standing, her head still bent.

Hamish turned and walked away and let himself out into the night.

Hamish's first visitor early next morning was Jamie Ross. 'I don't know whether I'm doin' the right thing or not,' said Jamie. 'I got back last night and found everything in order, but no sign of Sandy. I went out to his place, but there was no one home.'

'Maybe he's indoors, dead drunk, and cannae hear you,' said Hamish.

'No, the door wasn't locked. I took a look inside. He's gone all right, but his Land Rover's still there. I'm wondering whether to report him missing.'

'It's early days,' said Hamish. 'Had he been drinking?'

'Well, that's what worries me. He had. Worse than that, he told Hector at The Clachan that I had kindly left a glass of booze for him on one of the tanks. I wouldn't dream of doing a thing like that. Hector said he was drinking himself silly. I got mad and asked why no one had stopped him. But far from stopping him, the locals seem to have gone out of their way to buy him drinks.'

'Why would they do that?'

'Jealousy,' said Jamie simply. 'You know what they're like around here. They don't like me showing I have any money at all. You're supposed to be like the crofters and plead poverty. That's why a lot of these crofters don't buy their land, you know. They could force the landowner to sell it to them for a song, but then that'd mean they'd need to pass a means test in order to get the government grants, and not one of them could pass it. Sandy's a good soul when he's not drinking. I'd hate to see him have an accident. It would be just like him to wander off and fall asleep somewhere and die of exposure. Besides, I owed him the second half of his wages and it's strange he didn't turn up to collect. He went away and left the office locked up and took the key with him. I had to break in.'

'I'll have a look around,' said Hamish. 'So you think someone deliberately left that drink so as Sandy would go on drinking, once started?'

'Aye, sheer spite.'

'I'll do my best. How was the wedding?'

'Oh, just grand. Everything went off like clockwork. They're off to the Canary Islands on their honeymoon.'

When Jamie left, Hamish washed his breakfast dishes and prepared to go out to look for Sandy Carmichael. He was on the point of leaving when Jenny arrived, looking shamefaced.

'Thanks for last night,' she said awkwardly. 'I wasn't myself.'

'That's all right,' said Hamish. 'I was just on my road out. Jamie Ross says that Sandy Carmichael is missing. But there's time for a coffee. You wouldn't happen to know if Sandy's ever gone missing before?'

'Not that I know. Drunk or sober, he always hangs about the town. Oh, here's Mrs

Mainwaring,' said Jenny, spotting a massive figure passing the kitchen window. 'I wonder what she wants.'

Hamish went through to the police station annexe in time to open the door to Mrs Mainwaring.

She was wearing a squashed felt hat and a waxed coat over a navy dress with a white sailor collar, a photograph of which had appeared several months ago in one of the Sunday colour supplements: 'Order now. Special offer. Flattering to the fuller figure.' A strong smell of peppermint and whisky blasted into Hamish's face as she cried, 'William is missing. He hasn't been home for two nights!'

'Come in, Mrs Mainwaring,' said Hamish. 'Sit yourself down.'

Jenny came through and stood in the office doorway. 'What's the matter?' she asked.

'Mr Mainwaring is missing,' said Hamish. 'Look, Mrs Mainwaring, has he done this before?'

'No, never. I mean, yes, he has, but he's always told me or left a note.'

'And where does he go?'

'Glasgow or Edinburgh. He likes to go to the theatre.'

'Alone?'

'Yes, of course.'

Hamish thought that William Mainwaring

86

might possibly have a mistress in Glasgow or Edinburgh – either that or be staying away out of sheer malice. 'I think you should give it a little more time,' he said soothingly. 'He'll be back.'

Jenny came forward and stood with her hand on Mrs Mainwaring's shoulder. 'And I think you ought to look for him,' she said sharply. 'Can't you see how distressed Mrs Mainwaring is?'

'All right,' said Hamish reluctantly. 'I've got to look for Sandy Carmichael, and so I may as well look for Mr Mainwaring at the same time.'

Ian Gibb was a budding reporter. He was on the dole, but he scoured the countryside in the hope of a good story. Occasionally one of the Scottish newspapers used a short piece from him, but he dreamt of having a scoop, a story that would hit the London papers.

That day, his sights were lower. With all the fuss about the decline in educational standards, he had decided to write a feature on Cnothan School. The school was run on the lines of an old-fashioned village school. It taught all ages up to university level. Education standards were high and discipline was strict. Teachers wore black academic gowns in the classroom and mortar-boards on speech days. The headmaster, John Finch, was an ageing martinet, the type of headmaster of whom people approve after they have left school and do not have to endure being taught by such a rigid personality themselves.

The headmaster had agreed to see him, but, true to his type, planned to keep Ian kicking his heels outside the headmaster's study for a full quarter of an hour.

Ian was moodily wishing he could light up a cigarette. He was sitting on a hard bench with his back against the wall. But after five minutes of waiting, he was joined by a teenage girl. 'Hallo,' said Ian cheerfully. 'In trouble?'

'Oh, no,' said the girl. 'I am one of the school prefects, and Mrs Billings, the English teacher, has sent me along to report that two of the girls are misbehaving in class. I'll wait till you're finished.'

'Maybe you'd better go first,' said Ian, feeling disappointed in this girl, whose Highland beauty had initially charmed him. There was something cold-bloodedly precise about her manner. 'I'll be a while. I'm interviewing Mr Finch for my newspaper.'

'Which newspaper is that?'

Ian didn't have a newspaper, being a freelance. He only hoped one of them would take his education article. But he said, *The Scotsman,*' hoping to impress.

'Oh, that's why he's seeing you,' said the girl sedately. '*The Scotsman*'s a good paper. I didn't think he'd want to see a reporter, mind. I thought he would call it sensationalism.'

'What? Education?'

'No, the witchcraft story.'

Ian stiffened. 'Oh yes, that,' he said casually, although it was the first he had heard of it, as he lived in Dornoch. 'Bad business.'

'I don't approve of it myself,' said the girl primly. 'But there's no doubt in anyone's mind the Mainwarings were asking for it.'

There came a commotion from the end of the corridor. Ian took out a small notebook, and as the girl turned her head away, he rapidly scribbled down 'Mainwaring'. A harassed, middle-aged woman came along the corridor, dragging two weeping six-year-olds. She saw the girl and said, 'Gemma, was there ever such a business! These two brats were supposed to be off school with the flu. Now they say they were playing up on the moors and there's a skeleton in the middle of that ring of standing stones.'

She knocked sharply on the door of the headmaster's study, and, without waiting for a reply, she went in, dragging the weeping children behind her.

Ian pressed his ear against the panels of the door, 'Here!' cried the girl called Gemma. 'You cannae do that. I'll tell on you!'

'Go tell,' snarled Ian over his shoulder, and then he listened hard.

By the time Hamish Macbeth arrived at the ring of standing stones, there was already quite a large crowd gathered. His police Land Rover had been stopped by other cars and pedestrians, all crying to him about the skeleton up on the moors.

The crowd parted to let him through. The skeleton lay in all its horrible whiteness under a bleak windy sky.

Hamish walked forward and knelt down by the skeleton. The whiteness of the bone depressed him. He had been hoping it would turn out to be another joke, that it would prove to be a skeleton used by medical students, but this one was too new.

'I'm Dr Brodie,' said a red-haired man, coming up to join him. 'Is this a joke?'

'I hope so,' said Hamish. 'But I don't think so. What do you make of it?'

The doctor knelt down beside him and took out a strong magnifying glass. 'I've no doubt the pathologist will tell us soon enough, but I'm baffled.' He raised the skull gently and lay down with his head on the ground and peered at the back of it. 'Aye,' he murmured, 'whoever it was had his neck broken. It'll come away in your hands if you're not careful. And see here . . .' He pointed to the left arm bone. 'There's tiny scratches all over the bone.'

'Acid?'

'No, definitely not acid.' He sat back on his heels. 'Mainwaring's missing, isn't he?'

'Aye,' said Hamish, 'and Sandy Carmichael. Teeth. What about teeth?'

The doctor peered at the skull. 'None at all,' he said gloomily. 'Can't be Carmichael. I happen to know he had his own teeth. I don't know about Mainwaring. He never consulted me. Went to some doctor in Edinburgh.'

Hamish glanced round anxiously at the swelling crowd. 'I'll need help,' he said urgently. 'While I phone, you pick out the most reliable from the crowd and get them to find ropes and groundsheets. I want the whole place roped off and groundsheets over as much of the area surrounded by the stones as you can manage.'

When Hamish returned after using the car phone in the Land Rover, the doctor and his helpers were busy spreading tarpaulins over the turf.

Hamish's heart was beating hard. After that business on Clachan Mohr, he had hoped never to be the butt of a practical joke again, but he found he was praying that this would turn out to be one. But the sky was dark and windy and his Highland soul felt menace in the very air.

91

He took out his notebook and began to make rapid shorthand notes.

Then he was approached by a group of men and women – reporters from the *Northern Times*, *Highland Times*, Moray Firth Radio, and the *Ross-shire Journal*, all clamouring to know about witchcraft in Cnothan.

His heart sank. It was like a bad dream. He knew that the Glasgow and Edinburgh newspapers would soon follow, then the television teams, then the London newspaper and television reporters. But, worst of all – once more he would be working for Detective Chief Inspector Blair of Strathbane.

Ian Gibb had found his scoop at last.

Chapter Five

What makes life dreary is the want of motive.
— George Eliot

The circus came to town. All of it. The television crews with cables twisting like black snakes, the reporters, the feature writers, the photographers, the forensic team, squads of policemen to search for clues, and the fat, pompous figure of Chief Detective Inspector Blair among the lot.

Blair was determined to solve this case all on his own, without his thunder being stolen by that lanky village idiot, Hamish Macbeth, and so he told Hamish to 'run along' and keep the gentlemen of the press in order.

Hamish derived much better amusement from the spectacle of the press trying to winkle a comment out of the taciturn locals. It was Diarmuid Sinclair of all people who broke the ice. Driven out of Cnothan in the search for a friendlier interviewee, Grampian Television had come across Diarmuid in his fields. Since he had started to talk to Hamish Macbeth, there was no stopping Diarmuid. He talked and talked. He told fantastic Highland stories of witchcraft in Cnothan. He even said he believed there was a coven of witches in the town.

Diarmuid burst upon the six o'clock news and caused emerald-green jealousy in Cnothan. By evening the press were almost besieged by locals dying to be interviewed.

Hamish felt restless. Blair and his sidekicks, detectives Jimmy Anderson and Harry Mac-Nab, were cluttering up the police station, and one of the forensic team had commandeered the Land Rover. Hamish put Towser on the leash and ambled down to The Clachan. He felt if he could find the whereabouts of Sandy Carmichael, he might find the whereabouts of William Mainwaring and the identity of the skeleton. Mrs Mainwaring had tearfully confirmed her husband had false teeth, but it was hard to think of the means by which Mainwaring could have been reduced to bare bones so quickly.

It was pitch-black although it was only four in the afternoon, and the endless screaming wind of Sutherland was tearing at his clothes. The bar was closed but he could see a light inside and hammered on the door. After a wait of a few minutes, it was opened by Hector

94

Gunn. 'Mair questions,' he groaned when he saw Hamish. 'If it isnae the press, it's the polis. Come in.' Hamish went into the bar, which smelled of stale beer and strong disinfectant, with Towser at his heels.

'I want to know what happened when Sandy Carmichael was in here on Saturday evening,' said Hamish.

'Nothing happened. He drank himself stupid, that's all.'

'The man is a known alcoholic. Didn't you think buying him drinks was a form o' murder?' said Hamish.

'Och, I wouldnae say he was an alcoholic. Jist owerfond o' his dram.'

Hamish looked at Hector Gunn in silence. Was there any point in saying that a man who had the DTs with remarkable regularity was obviously not a social drinker? He decided it would be a waste of time.

'Well,' said Hamish, 'Let's put it another way. Who was the keenest to buy Sandy drinks?'

'I wasnae watching, and I've got mair to dae with ma time,' said Hector huffily. 'It was your job tae be doon here, seeing that none of them tried to drive when they had mair than enough. It was a noisy evening. Alistair Gunn, ma cousin, was in, and Dougie Macdonald. Something Mainwaring had said to Alistair was fair making him mad, although

95

he wouldnae say what it was. He wanted a crowd of them to debag Mainwaring and throw him in the loch. They were all as fierce as lions and saying what they were going to do to Mainwaring when in he walks and they all fall silent and become sheepish and shuffle their feet and not a word is said to the man. John Sinclair and his wife, Mary, came in and Mainwaring joined them, although they didn't want him to. Then that reporter, Ian Gibb, him from Dornoch, he was in, noisy and drunk, and Mainwaring leaves the Sinclairs and says something to him, and Gibb tries to punch him but falls on the floor. Then thae two crofters, Alec Birrell and Davey Macdonald, start shouting at Mainwaring that he's stealing good croft land from the crofters and Mainwaring tells them to get stuffed. Then Harry Mackay puts his oar in and says Mainwaring bought those houses and left them empty out o' spite, and Mainwaring says Mackay couldn't get a fuck in a brothel, he was that weak. Mackay walks off in a temper. I had a lot of customers to serve but I was just about to go around the bar and stop the noise when Mainwaring left and everything quietened down after that and they were all laughing at Sandy, who was standing on his chair and trying to do an impersonation of Frank Sinatra. I asked him for his car keys but he said he didnae have his Land Rover with him.'

Hamish asked a few more questions and then went off into the blackness of late afternoon. He decided to go out to the Cnothan Game and Fish Company to see if Jamie had heard any news of Sandy. He let Towser off the leash as soon as he was clear of the town traffic, and then he ambled along, whistling in a kind of dreary way.

Towser plunged into the fields on either side of the road, looking for rabbits. Hamish kept calling him back, shining his powerful torch across the fields. It was just when Towser had been gone some time and Hamish was wondering whether the dog had been caught in a rabbit trap, that he at last saw Towser loping back towards the road, his eyes gleaming in the long beam thrown by the torch.

'It's no use grinning at me like that,' grumbled Hamish, 'I've had enough. Back on the leash you go.'

And then Towser's absurd grin slipped and fell to the grass. Wondering, Hamish bent down and shone his torch on a set of false teeth. He took out a clean handkerchief and picked them up.

'Where did you get this, boy?' he whispered. 'Over there? Come on. Show me!'

Towser obediently trotted off, stopping and turning every few yards to make sure his master was following him. 'Fetch!' called Hamish when Towser finally stopped and pawed the ground. Towser scoured around, bringing back everything he could find, from rusty tin cans to old shoes. Hamish turned and looked back. There was a car going along the road, not far away. As he watched, the car window opened and something came hurtling out. He walked forward and looked. It was a crushed beer can.

He stood in the darkness, shivering in the wind, and thinking hard.

He shone his torch on the false teeth. They were stained with nicotine.

He wrapped them carefully in his handkerchief again and began to make his way back to the road. He put Towser back on the leash and headed on towards the Game and Fish Company.

As he reached the yard, Jamie cruised in in his white Mercedes with his wife. The floodlights in the yard were switched on and so Hamish was able to view Jamie's wife clearly. She was a tall, slim Highland beauty with masses of jet-black hair, a creamy skin, and a luscious mouth. She was wearing a mink coat open over a white shirt blouse and jeans and black leather boots with very high stiletto heels.

Jamie introduced her, and then said, 'We'll be in the office, Helen, if you want me.'

His wife smiled vaguely and then swayed off in the direction of the house.

'Now, what can I do for you?' asked Jamie. 'Found Sandy?'

'No,' said Hamish. 'I was hoping you would have had some news.'

Jamie led the way into the office. 'That's a funny-looking police dog,' he said, looking at Towser.

'Aye,' said Hamish, not wanting to explain that Towser was a pet and not a trained blood-hound. He often felt half-ashamed of his affection for the animal.

'It's a funny business this,' said Jamie. 'The skeleton, I mean. It can't be Sandy or Main-waring. No acid, they say. Maybe the flesh was boiled off.'

'The bones were too hard,' said Hamish vaguely. 'Let me see that lobster shed again, Jamie. I'd like to see if I can find any clue as to who left the whisky there. I was called out to the Angler's Rest on Saturday evening and it turned out to be a hoax. It's all connected. I tried to tell Blair, but he wouldnae listen.'

'That man never listens to anyone,' said Jamie. 'Come on, and I'll show you the shed again.'

Hamish looked down into the centre lobster tank. It was empty and the water was still. 'Be getting another load in soon,' said Jamie, 'but the weather's terrible bad.'

Taking out his torch, Hamish switched it on and began to search in the dark corners.

'Look here, Hamish,' said Jamie crossly. 'I didn't like Mainwaring, but if you think I bumped him off and fed him to the lobsters –'

He broke off. Hamish straightened up and turned and looked at Jamie, his hazel eyes blank.

'Aye, chust so,' he said. And then he continued searching again.

Jamie waited and fidgeted and then burst out with, 'I've got more to do than stand here on a cold night watching you playing yourself, Hamish. I'm going to join the wife. Shut the shed door after you when you're finished.'

Hamish grunted. He was down on his hands and knees on the floor, the top of his peaked cap just visible over the concrete edge of the tank.

Jamie snorted with disgust and went off. Hamish crawled around the tank, examining the edges and the floor, inch by inch. Towser kept leaping on him, thinking it was some sort of game, and Hamish kept having to push the dog away.

On the far side of the tank, away from the door, there was a thin crack in the concrete side. In the crack was a limp, damp strand of red wool. Hamish fished in his pockets until he found a pair of tweezers. He carefully extracted the strand of wool and held it up to the light. Then he sat down suddenly on the floor with his back to the tank, his mind racing.

100

He thought about the skeleton, about the newness of it, about the scratches and scores on the bone. He carefully tucked the strand away in a clean envelope. He got to his feet, noticing as he did so in a detached kind of way that his knees were trembling.

He made his way out and over to Jamie's house, a long, low bungalow that made up the south side of the square yard, the three sheds with the office alongside one of the sheds making up the other three sides.

He rang the bell. The strains of 'Loch Lomond' chimed out into the night. Jamie answered the door. 'Just away, are you, Hamish?'

Hamish shook his head sadly. 'No, I have to talk to ye.'

'Well, come in, but leave that dog in the kitchen. The wife won't thank you for muddy paws on her carpets.'

He led the way through the kitchen and into the living-room. Kitchen or back doors are always used in the Highlands. The front door is used only for carrying out the coffin at funerals and for New Year's Eve parties.

The sitting-room was brilliantly lit by a chandelier on the low ceiling. It had been made for a much bigger room with a much higher ceiling, and Hamish ducked his head under it as he went to sit down on the edge of a white leather sofa. Helen Ross smiled at him vaguely and went back to turning the pages of a copy of *Vogue*. The carpet was white too, Hamish noticed. Despite his distress, he found himself wondering how old Helen Ross was. With a grown-up son, she was in her late thirties at least, but she seemed peculiarly ageless.

'Now, what's the trouble, man?' said Jamie, sitting down on a white leather armchair opposite Hamish.

'Where are all those lobsters that you had at the weekend?' asked Hamish.

Jamie looked surprised. 'Let me see ... the lads had just packed the trucks and were ready to drive off when I came back on Sunday night. I got the last train, five o'clock from Inverness, which got in about eight-thirty.'

'Didn't you take the car?'

'No, I don't like to drive all that way in winter. I left it at Cnothan station.'

'And the lobsters will be sold by now?'

'Sold, cooked, and eaten. They were in the market in Billingsgate first thing this morning.'

'But there'll be some in the shops?' asked Hamish with a note of desperation in his voice.

'I doubt it. Restaurants, big hotels, even the House of Commons. Maybe Harrods will have some, of course.'

Hamish put his head in his hands and groaned.

Jamie looked at him in silence and then he said slowly, 'Are you trying to say that that skeleton was because of my lobsters?'

'It looks like that, Jamie.'

Jamie went white to the lips. 'It cannae be. No, I won't believe it.'

'You know thae lobsters could clean a corpse of flesh and they'd have had the bones too if the skeleton hadn't been fished out.'

'Hamish,' said Jamie. 'This is a matter of life and death.'

Helen Ross gave a delicate yawn and rustled the pages of the magazine.

'It's a case o' murder,' said Hamish Macbeth.

'But this could ruin me. It will ruin me,' cried Jamie. 'Don't you see? Those lobsters'll be eaten by all the top people in London and it'll be in the papers that Jamie Ross turned them all into cannibals! Hush it up, man. How much?'

'Jamie, you're no' dreamin' o' bribing me!' exclaimed Hamish.

'Not you in particular. The police. They always want funds for something.'

'It won't do,' said Hamish mournfully.

Jamie raised his fists. 'That bastard, Mainwaring. I don't think it was murder at all. I think the bastard was poking about and fell in the tank and struck his head or something. Maybe he committed suicide to spite me.'

'We don't know yet that it was Mainwaring,' said Hamish.

'Who else would cause such trouble?' said Jamie.

Hamish rose to his feet and looked down at Jamie sadly. 'I have to ask you to seal off that shed and not to use it until it's had a thorough going-over.'

'I'm ruined,' whispered Jamie. 'Ruined.'

His wife rose to her feet in one elegant fluid movement. She went to a drinks trolley in the corner, poured a stiff whisky, and then handed the glass to her husband. Then she sat down again and picked up a gold cigarette case from a side table.

She took out a cigarette and lit it with a solid gold lighter. Then she looked at her husband.

'You'll be as famous as Sweeney Todd,' she said in a soft Highland voice. 'Chust think of that!' And then she laughed.

Hamish trudged back into Cnothan with Towser at his heels. He should have used Jamie's phone and summoned the police immediately. But he wanted to think. He would like to do something to save Jamie's business. But Jamie might be a murderer. His thoughts went round and round and always came back to focus on Priscilla Halburton-Smythe. He had heard about addicts trying to give up drink or drugs who managed well for a bit and then some piece of worry or distress would set up the old craving again. And so Hamish Macbeth craved Priscilla.

At that very moment, Priscilla was thinking about Hamish instead of paying attention to her date. She had been startled to see and hear the story of witchcraft in Cnothan on the six-o'clock news. There had been a brief shot of a group of policemen and detectives, and there, on the edge of the group, had stood Hamish Macbeth. He looked lost, ill at ease, and a bit silly. I hope Blair isn't giving him a hard time, thought Priscilla.

The restaurant she was in was crowded. It was society's latest 'find'. Priscilla did not like it one bit. It was full of Hooray Henrys and their Henriettas, all being familiar with the waiters, which had resulted in the Italian waiters' being noisy and insolent, rather in the way that top hairdressers are encouraged to be insolent by that masochistic streak in the English upper class.

Priscilla was helping a girlfriend to run a hat shop in the King's Road in Chelsea. The girlfriend, Sarah Paterson, was convinced that hats were about to make a come-back. Priscilla had promised Sarah to help her out for six months. Now she was wishing she had never made such a promise. The shop was usually full of people giggling and trying on hats, but very few bought any, and some days their only sales seemed to be made to transvestites whose idea of fashion had stayed frozen in the fifties.

I would be better off in Lochdubh minding Hamish's sheep for him, Priscilla's thoughts ran on. I wonder who he got to look after things? I'm surprised Blair allowed him near Cnothan. Maybe he was only there for the day. She had a sudden yearning to be in Hamish's cluttered kitchen, to sit and gossip about local things while Towser snored at their feet and the wind howled down the loch. She realized her dinner date, Jeremy Tring-Gillingham, was speaking to her.

'You made a great mistake in not having the lobster, Priscilla,' said Jeremy. 'Mario tells me he goes down to Billingsgate first thing to buy everything fresh. The taste is exquisite.'

'Mmm,' said Priscilla. 'Have you been following that story, Jeremy, the one on the news this evening, about witchcraft in Sutherland?'

'Oh, that,' mumbled Jeremy, swallowing more lobster. 'Sounds great, but you'll find it was probably some medical students playing about.'

Blair and Hamish were closeted in the police-station annexe. Hamish had insisted they be alone. The pair of false teeth and the little

106

strand of scarlet wool lay on the desk between them.

'So,' said Blair savagely, when Hamish had finished, 'instead o' picking up the phone, you great gowk, you takes your doggie fur a walk back here to tell me. Jist keep out of it while I take MacNab and Anderson down there and arrest Ross.'

'He wasnae there at the time, or as far as we know,' said Hamish. 'He was at his son's wedding in Inverness. Mind you, we'll need to make sure he was there the whole time. He's got a powerful car. He may not have left it in the station car park like he said. You'll look damned silly if you arrest him and then have to let him off, and a man like Jamie Ross would have you in court for causing him undue distress and everything else he could throw at you. And there's one big thing you'd better think of before you tell anyone of this.'

'Whit's that, Sherlock?' demanded Blair sarcastically.

'Jamie Ross's lobsters go to all the top places in London and even to the House of Commons dining room. Think about it! "Prime Minister a Cannibal." Can't you see the headlines? The scandal will be terrible, and someone's head is going to have to roll for letting those lobsters go off to London. Oh, I know, there wasnae time to stop them, but the big ones will want a sacrifice, and they're not going to take their temper out on a mere village copper. So that leaves you.'

Blair, who had half-risen to his feet, sank back in his chair.

'Get oot o' here,' he snarled, 'and keep your mouth shut.'

He picked up the phone and began to dial an Inverness number.

Hamish strolled over to Jenny's cottage and knocked on the door. 'Come in,' she said, answering it promptly. 'Have you eaten?'

'No, I've been ordered out the police station by Blair.'

'Horrible man,' said Jenny. 'I can feed you and Towser. How's the investigation going?'

'Something pretty terrible's come up,' said Hamish. 'It looks as if that skeleton was Mainwaring's after all.'

'But it can't be!' said Jenny. 'How?'

'I can't tell ye,' said Hamish. 'It's all very puzzling. Are you all right?' he added sharply, for Jenny was very white.

'I'm fine, fine.' She sat down and looked at her hands.

'Your sister's death must still be troubling ye sore,' said Hamish sympathetically.

'I hated her,' said Jenny fiercely.

Embarrassed and not knowing quite how to react, Hamish began to speak aloud about the crime. 'It's the lack of a motive that puzzles me,' he said half to himself. 'A lot of people

hated Mainwaring, but only enough to per-
petrate some piece of spite. I wonder whether
it was a practical joke that went wrong?'

Jenny got to her feet and took two steaks
out of the refrigerator. Towser placed a large
yellow paw with ludicrous familiarity on her
bottom. She shrugged and took out another
steak and went to a small microwave oven in
the corner.

'How does your dog like his steak done?'
she asked over her shoulder.

'Well done,' said Hamish absent-mindedly,
'and the same for me.' He returned to musing
aloud. 'Yes, when you look at it first, there
seem to be a lot of suspects, but not one of
them the killer type. There chust isn't a
strong-enough motive. Not for this kind of
killing. Not for all the wicked cruelty of it.
Someone must have had nerves of steel to kill
the man and then –' He broke off. The lobsters
must stay secret.

'That's enough about murder,' he said.
'Have you been painting?'

'No, I haven't been in the mood. Any news
of Sandy?'

'Not a word as far as I know. But then I'm
being kept out o' the investigation. Most of my
day was taken up listening to residents' complaints about the press.'

'You've worked with Blair before, haven't
you? There were those two murders over in

Lochdubh. You're a sort of vulture, Hamish Macbeth. Murder follows you around wherever you go.'

'Don't say that.' Hamish shuddered. 'I suppose it will have been on the national news.'

'Bound to be,' said Jenny. 'Nothing else is happening, although the networks don't seem to have caught on to the fact that the great British public has really no interest in foreign news whatsoever. They probably gave it two minutes after a long speech from Reagan, a longer one from Gorbachev, and practically a whole fifteen minutes on the riots in Paris.'

'So people in London would see it,' said Hamish. Had *she* seen it? And would it prompt her to return?

'So who's in London that you want to remind of your existence?' said Jenny, her slate-coloured eyes suddenly shrewd.

Hamish blushed and looked away. 'Ma cousin Rory. He's a reporter.'

'On Fleet Street?'

'I don't think there's a reporter left in Fleet Street,' said Hamish. 'Rory has moved to Docklands like everyone else. I was hoping he would be up. I would have phoned him, but Blair's crouched over the police phone like a great toad.'

'Go and use mine,' said Jenny, tossing salad in a bowl. 'You'll find it through in the living-room.'

110

The living-room was actually the gallery. There were easy chairs and a coffee-table. Jenny hardly ever used it herself except when working or entertaining prospective customers. There was a painting, a view of Clachan Mohr, on an easel. Hamish recognized that odd cliff which he had climbed when Alistair and Dougie had played that trick on him. That he recognized it did not surprise him. All Jenny's paintings were representational. But it was the power in the picture, the black and boiling sky above the sinister cliff, the stark trees and bleak landscape beyond. He lightly touched the paint with his finger. Wet. And yet she'd said she had not been painting. And she had never painted with such power and ferocity before.

He phoned his cousin on the *Daily Recorder*, marvelling, not for the first time, how long it took the newspaper's switchboard to answer the call. He was told that Rory was in Paris, covering the riots.

'Is that a fact,' said Hamish cosily. He was addicted to gossipy long-distance calls. 'And why is it your Paris office isn't covering it?'

'The Paris office was closed down last year,' said the reporter at the other end. 'Who is calling?'

'This is Police Constable Macbeth. Rory's cousin.'

111

'Oh, you're the one in the Highlands. Hold on a minute, till I switch on the recorder. I'd better have a word with you about this witchcraft murder.'

'I cannae say anything. Phone Chief Detective Inspector Blair at Cnothan 252,' said Hamish and dropped the receiver.

'Your steak's ready,' said Jenny when he returned to the kitchen. 'What do I do about Towser? Does he like a knife and fork?'

'I spoil him,' said Hamish awkwardly. 'Put his steak beside me and I'll cut it up for him.'

'I haven't any wine,' said Jenny apologetically.

'I hae a bottle in the station,' said Hamish. 'I'll be back in a minute if I can get it without Blair seeing me.'

He ran out and across the road, keeping to the grass at the side of the short driveway so that his boots would not crunch on the gravel. He peered into the lounge. Blair, MacNab, and Anderson were sitting there, talking earnestly, their feet up on the glass table.

Hamish crept into the kitchen and opened the cupboard where he had put the bottle of wine. He was just about to escape when he heard Blair's voice approaching. He jumped into the broom cupboard and closed the door behind him.

He could hear the noise of the fridge door being opened and then a hiss as Blair opened a can of beer. My beer, thought Hamish furiously.

'While we sort this thing out and wait for instructions from Inverness,' Blair shouted through to his sidekicks, 'we'll send Macbeth down to Mrs Mainwaring with thae teeth.'

'Where is he?' Anderson's voice came faintly.

'Bonking that artist over the road.'

Blair's voice faded as he went back into the lounge and closed the door.

Hamish got out of the cupboard and out of the kitchen as fast as he could. He was determined his evening with Jenny Lovelace was not going to be spoiled. He ran into Jenny's living-room and seized the phone and dialled the police-station number. After a few moments, Detective Jimmy Anderson answered it.

'Murder!' screamed Hamish in a high falsetto voice. 'Sandy Carmichael is attacking me with the meat cleaver. Murder! Oh, help. This is Jeannie at the Angler's Rest.'

He put down the phone and went to the window. Blair, Anderson, and MacNab rushed out and climbed into the Land Rover and shot off with the siren blaring.

Hamish grinned. If they thought they had got their man, they would not want Hamish Macbeth there to share in any part of the glory.

'What's all the commotion?' asked Jenny when he entered the kitchen. 'Your steak's getting cold.'

'I don't know,' said Hamish innocently. 'Here's the wine.'

They had a companionable meal. Hamish washed the dishes and then politely took Jenny's hand to thank her for the meal and say good night. He didn't know quite how it happened, but the next moment she was pressed against him and a moment after that he was kissing her passionately.

Towser watched in amazement as the trail of clothes up the stairs to Jenny's bedroom lengthened. A pair of regulation police trousers sailed down from the top and landed on Towser's nose. He snuffled at them dismally and then curled up on the trousers and went to sleep.

At midnight, Blair knocked furiously on the door. Towser raised his head and sniffed the air, and then lowered it on to Hamish's trousers and went back to sleep. He knew Blair as well as his master did.

Chapter Six

Jenny kissed me when we met,
Jumping from the chair she sat in;
Time, you thief who love to get
Sweets into your list, put that in:
Say I'm weary, say I'm sad,
Say that health and wealth have missed me,
Say I'm growing old, but add,
Jenny kissed me.
                    – James Henry Leigh Hunt

Hamish awoke at dawn the next morning, dazed, bewildered, and happy. He would have liked to cuddle up to Jenny and spend the lazy morning in bed, but he did not want her to become the butt of Blair's coarse remarks, and so he dressed quickly, picking up items of clothing from the stairs, and finally rescuing his trousers from under Towser.

He made his way quietly over to the police station and was just emerging innocent from his own bedroom when Blair came looking for him.

'Where was ye last night?' howled Blair. 'Getting your leg over that artist bint?'

'I wass out looking for clues,' said Hamish. 'Miss Lovelace is a highly respectable lady. I am furthermore quite prepared to put my job on the line if you make any more filthy remarks about her by sinking ma fist right into your mouth.'

Blair backed before the fury in Hamish's eyes. 'Cannae ye take a joke?' he said. 'Me and the others are off to stay at the Anstey Hotel doon the road. The bigwigs are comin' up from Inverness and Edinburgh to see what we can do about keeping thae lobsters quiet. In the meantime, you take those false teeth down to Mrs Mainwaring and let's hear what she says.'

Blair walked into the lounge as he talked. Hamish looked around the room in dismay. The ashtrays were overflowing, and there were greasy fish-and-chip papers on the coffee table.

'And what am I supposed to do about this mess?' asked Hamish.

'Oh, get a wumman in tae clean the place and put the bill through the expenses as something else.'

Furious as he was at the state of the place, Hamish was only too glad to get rid of Blair

116

and his detectives. It meant he would have the phone to himself again.

He got into the police Land Rover and drove off before Blair could commandeer it. It would be just like Blair to expect him to walk the miles to Mrs Mainwaring's.

And before he even reached Mrs Mainwaring, he had to quieten his conscience by looking for Sandy Carmichael. The moors were covered with searching policemen, but there might be something he, Hamish Macbeth, could find that they could not. He could not in his heart believe Sandy responsible for the murder. He called at Sandy's cottage after scouring the highways and byways, only to retreat quickly as Blair's furious face appeared at the window.

On his way to Mrs Mainwaring, Hamish dropped in to see Diarmuid Sinclair. He nearly didn't recognize him, for Diarmuid had shaved off his long beard. 'Why the new image?' asked Hamish. 'Doing it for your public?'

'Aye, did you see me on the television?' said Diarmuid. 'Grand, that was. John took a video o' it and showed it to me and I thought I looked that old. Forbye, I'm off to Inverness soon to buy wee Sean a present for his birthday.' Sean was Diarmuid's grandson. 'Have ye any idea what I should get?'

'How old is he?'

'Eight.'

'Well,' said Hamish, 'I would just buy the bairn something you would like to play with yourself.'

He then drove on to the Mainwaring bungalow.

Mrs Mainwaring was packing clothes, boxes and boxes of them. There were no men's clothes among the piles lying ready for packing, but Hamish recognized the blue-and-white sailor dress. She was obviously getting rid of all the clothes her husband had chosen for her. Mrs Mainwaring believed her husband was dead.

'What can I do for you, officer?' she asked, as she competently went on with her packing, a cigarette drooping from her lips.

'Can you identify these? Don't touch them.' Hamish took out the false teeth, enclosed in a polythene bag. She went very still. She took the cigarette from her mouth and tossed it into the fire.

'They're William's,' she said flatly. 'He had them specially made, complete with nicotine stains, so they would not look too white and too false.' She sat down, her baggy tweed skirt rucked up, displaying large areas of muscled thigh.

'I'll take a statement from ye,' said Hamish gently. 'And then maybe you could call by later in the day at the police station and sign it.'

She nodded. 'Where did you find them?'

118

'My dog found them in that patch of scrub at the turn of the road outside Cnothan as you go out toward Cnothan Game.'

'I knew he was dead,' she said dully. 'I felt it. He wouldn't have left me alone this long. He liked tormenting me too much. Poor William.'

'Mrs Mainwaring, if that skeleton is your husband's, have you any idea what might have happened to him?'

'No. I don't like to think about it. It can't be his. I don't think it's anything to do with him. It was put there for a bad joke.'

Hamish looked at her curiously. She seemed quite calm, but shock affected people in strange ways.

'Would it upset you to talk to me about him?' he asked gently. 'Tell me about his army career. He said he had something to do with MI5.'

'Told you that one, did he?' Mrs Mainwaring lit another cigarette. 'He liked to play the retired army man, part of his act. He was a captain when he did his National Service. He was never a career officer. He just got drafted along with everyone else.'

'And how did he make his money?'

She gave a horrible kind of laugh. 'He married me,' she said. 'I was living in Maidstone in Kent with my mother, who was on her last legs. No man had ever proposed to me or looked at me, and then William came along.' Her eyes grew dreamy. 'He was selling cars. Mother used to make nasty jokes about car salesmen and said he was only after my money. I didn't believe her. He had very great charm. But I should have seen through him then. I told him Mother held the purse-strings and after that I didn't see him for a week. At the end of that week, Mother died of a heart attack, the death was published in the local paper, and William came back again, just in time for the funeral. He was very supportive. He said he had inherited an estate in Scotland. We would be married and go and live there.

'Mother left me the house in Maidstone and quite a bit of money. I was tired. I was old-fashioned. I had been led to believe that women did not have heads for business. William said if I transferred everything to him, he would arrange for the sale of the house and take care of everything.'

'That was verra trusting of you,' said Hamish awkwardly.

She went on as if he had not spoken. 'So I did, and we got married, and came up here to live. I know a lot of incomers don't like Cnothan, but I loved it, and I still do. The women were so pleasant and gentle and friendly. Old-fashioned, just like me. But William changed. I forgave him for lying, you know. This place is hardly an estate. He started nagging me and nagging me from morning till night. He hated this place, and he began to enjoy people hating him. It made him feel important. I couldn't walk out. He had control of the money.

'You've heard of the Duke of Sutherland, the one in the last century, who was responsible for the Highland Clearances – the one who had his factors drive the crofters out of their houses so he could turn the whole of the north into a sheep ranch?'

'Of course,' said Hamish.

'Well, you know how they still hate the duke in Sutherland. He had that statue of himself erected above Golspie and his memory is still so hated that people can't bear to look at it. That tickled William. He liked going for long walks. He would often walk to the top of Clachan Mohr. He used to say that one day he would get a statue of himself put up there.'

'And what is his family background?'

'Surprisingly good. Went to Marlborough, then New College, although he left after only two years without getting his degree. Went to work for a family friend in the City as a stock-broker after he did his National Service. After that, I don't know. He was always vague about it. But something happened. His family didn't come to the wedding. He has two sisters and a brother living. They won't have anything to do with him.'

'Have you their addresses?'

Mrs Mainwaring went over to a desk and fished out an address book. She copied out three addresses on to a slip of paper and handed it to Hamish.

'Can you put those bloody teeth away?' she said sharply.

Hamish put the polythene bag back in his pocket.

'You will inherit his money if he is dead, will you not?' asked Hamish.

'I'll get my own money back, if that's what you mean,' said Mrs Mainwaring drily.

'Now about those houses and crofts he bought,' said Hamish. 'What did he plan to do with them?'

'If you ask me, he planned to go on using the land for his sheep and let the houses rot. I pointed out time and again that he could sell the houses and keep the croft land, but he enjoyed the locals' fury. They hated him for letting two good houses stand there decaying. Somehow, he had led them to believe he hadn't much money. He worked hard in the beginning at getting everyone to like him. He wasn't a complete stranger. He had been up on visits before; this aunt was the only member of the family who still liked him. And so they accepted him as a crofter without question.'

'Now, Mrs Mainwaring, it takes a very strong motive to kill a man, that is, if your husband has been killed. Have you any idea who might have done it?'

'It could have been pretty much anybody,' she said. 'I can't help you there.'

Hamish asked several more questions, got the address in Edinburgh of the dentist who had supplied the false teeth, and then took his leave.

Mrs Mainwaring shook hands with him, waved goodbye, and as soon as the police Land Rover was out of sight, she sank down in a chair, holding her large body in her arms to stop the uncontrollable shaking.

As Hamish drove up to the Cnothan Game and Fish Company, he was stopped a few yards before he reached it by a police barrier behind which swarms of press were being held at bay. The barrier was raised to let him through. He saw the yard was full of plainclothes officers. Blair and several high-ranking policemen were watching the operations.

Blair saw Hamish approaching and went to meet him as Hamish's lanky figure descended from the Land Rover. Hamish grinned. Blair was determined that Hamish Macbeth should not meet any of the top brass.

'Did she recognize the teeth?' demanded Blair.

'Aye,' said Hamish. 'They're Mainwaring's all right. How's the big hush-up going?'

'It's going jist fine. Nobody's going to talk, least of all Jamie Ross.'

Hamish pushed back his cap and scratched his head thoughtfully. 'Have ye thought what's going to happen when you get your man, or woman, and he or she appears in the dock? What about the evidence? There'll be an even bigger scandal in the press if they find out you've been suppressing vital evidence.'

Blair went scarlet. His mind hadn't worked as far in advance as that.

'Don't you worry, sonny,' he growled. 'Leave important matters like that to the high-ups. Now, get back to that station and type up Mrs Mainwaring's statement.'

But instead of going to the station, Hamish drove back to Sandy's cottage. There was a strange policeman on duty. He shrugged when Hamish said he wanted to look around and said, 'Help yourself.'

Hamish pushed open the door and went in. Nothing, he reflected sadly, is more bleak than the home of a drunk. Unwashed dishes were piled high in the greasy sink. The wood-burning stove was black with old grease. The floor was covered with food and drink stains, the bedroom smelled appallingly. He poked about through closets, through piles of romances, through hidden stacks of empty bottles, but there was no clue to where Sandy could have gone. There were no personal papers, no clue to relatives – unless Blair had taken them away. He went out past the policeman and round to the back. The garden was a tip of old rubbish, old tyres, broken cups, more empty bottles, a shattered hen coop, and a large oil drum with holes bored in the side for burning refuse. Hamish tipped up the oil drum and looked inside. It was empty, but no doubt Forensic had taken away the contents to examine them. He was about to turn away when he noticed a blacker patch on the earth at his feet. He bent down and poked a finger into the soil. The ground was soft, as if it had recently been turned over and raked. He stood up and pushed his cap on the back of his head and thought hard. If Sandy had burnt something in the garden recently, something so important that he had taken the ashes and raked the ground, it followed that Sandy Carmichael could be the murderer. But Hamish still could not believe it.

When he left the cottage, he went on to where Clachan Mohr reared up against a milky-blue sky. It had turned mild, and a soft wind brought hope of spring. He suddenly remembered how Jenny's lips had felt pressed against his own and smiled. And yet to Hamish's old-fashioned way of thinking, there was something slightly sad about bed before courtship. He might have fallen in love with her. Not that he was a prude or thought that Jenny's morals were lax in any way. But in affairs, it was sometimes better to travel slowly than arrive too quickly. Instant gratification certainly knocked the spiritual side out of romance, no matter how much the modern mind tried to shout down the primitive emotions.

He parked the Land Rover and walked around a track at the foot of the cliff that led to the easy way up at the back. He walked steadily up the twisting track. At the top, a magnificent stag raised its head and stared at him with sad, wary eyes, like a schoolmaster surveying a tormenting schoolboy. Then it dipped its antlers and began to move off with that characteristically odd jerking start which quickly changed into the supple speed of a full gallop.

Hamish suddenly felt deliriously happy. The warm day, the stag, Jenny, the springy heather, Jenny, the sun on his neck, Jenny – all crowded together and sky-rocketed in his brain. He did several cartwheels across the springy heather and then fell on his back, laughing helplessly. His sadness about sleeping with Jenny had gone. He felt sure he loved her.

And then he longed for a cigarette. The Americans would call it the reward syndrome, he thought. Something good happens, and you deserve a treat. Surely the cleverest advertising slogan man ever created was 'Have Some Cadbury's, You Deserve It'.

He was clambering to his feet, reminding himself he was supposed to be looking for clues, when he saw a glimmer of white down under deep clumps of heather. He fished out two crumpled paper cups.

He turned them round and round in his hands. There was a smear of lipstick on one. He looked closer. No, it was not a smear of lipstick, it was a smudged fingerprint. Paint. Oil paint.

He sat down and put the cups carefully on the grass and looked at them.

A cloud swept across the sun and he shivered.

Paint.

Jenny.

Paint + paper cup = Jenny.

But it could have been a schoolchild.

There were traces of coffee in the bottom of the cup. Children these days did not drink tea or coffee. They drank Coke or 7-Up or Dr Pepper or a Scottish soda called Barr's Irn Bru, 'made from girders'.

He clutched his head. Time. Think about time. *Jenny had been crying on – when was it? Sunday. Her sister had died. She had received a letter. Funny, that. The police were usually informed. Wait a bit! Jenny could have been here with someone else. It need not have been Mainwaring. Oh God, let it not be Jenny.*

He searched further under the heather clumps and came up with a pipe. Mainwaring had smoked a pipe.

He picked up the cups and put them in a bag along with the pipe and carried them down from Clachan Mohr. He drove carefully back to the police station and then crossed the road to Jenny's cottage.

He did not even have time to knock. She opened the door even as he was raising his hand to the knocker. Her black hair was endearingly tousled and her lips were still slightly swollen from love-making.

'Hamish!' she cried. And then the light slowly left her eyes as she looked into his face. He silently held up the plastic bag containing the two crumpled cups and the pipe.

'I found these up on Clachan Mohr,' he said.

He brushed past her into the cottage. She followed him into the kitchen. 'Where's Towser?' she asked with a laugh that sounded false.

He sat down at the kitchen table and placed the bag with the cups in front of him.

'Now, Jenny,' he said quietly. 'For a start, let's see that letter from Canada. The one telling you about your sister's death.'

Jenny slid on to his knee and wrapped her

128

arms around his neck. 'Hamish!' she said. 'Don't turn detective on me.'

'The letter, Jenny,' said Hamish, his hazel eyes hard and bleak.

He lifted her up like a child and placed her on a seat next to his own.

'The letter,' he demanded again.

'I threw it away,' said Jenny.

'I can ask the postie if you got a letter from Canada and if he says you didn't get one, that will prove you're lying. Don't make me do that.'

'Oh, all right,' shouted Jenny. And then in a quieter, almost defeated tone of voice, she repeated, 'All right.'

'Tell me about it,' said Hamish gently.

Jenny shrugged. 'It's all so silly, really. There's nothing to tell. I was upset about my painting. I had doubts that I was any good, that I would ever be any good. I felt you wouldn't understand, no one would understand, and so I told that lie.'

'Were you Mainwaring's mistress?' asked Hamish brutally.

'No! Never! Damn you. You're like all men. The minute you've slept with them, they've damned you as a whore.'

'Wait a minute,' said Hamish.

He got to his feet and went through and looked at the oil painting of Clachan Mohr that stood in the gallery.

Jenny went for walks, he remembered. This painting shrieked rage and sorrow and menace. And yet none of Jenny's other paintings reflected anything at all. Powerful emotion had rocked her to the very foundations.

'Okay,' said Jenny's voice from behind him. 'I went for walks with William Mainwaring. I saw a side of him that no one else saw. He was charming and kind.'

'Mrs Mainwaring saw that side,' said Hamish. 'That was before he married her and got her to sign her money over to him.'

A dry sob answered him and he turned round and looked compassionately at Jenny's bent head and then back to the picture again.

'He could never stop being the know-all, could he, Jenny?' said Hamish. 'He was flattered to have a pretty woman going along with him on his walks. But he had books on art appreciation on his shelves. He just had to tell you what he thought of your painting and it was Canada and your husband all over again. You painted Clachan Mohr right after that. You told me you had had a death in the family, because to you it was a bereavement. Another man you had admired and trusted had jumped all over your soul.'

Jenny slumped down on the floor and began to cry.

'I'm sorry,' said Hamish. 'This is going to look to you like another betrayal. I have to tell Blair. I don't think you killed him, but I have to tell Blair. You can't keep anything in the Highlands quiet, and sooner or later someone is going to tell Blair you went for walks with Mainwaring.'

To Hamish's relief, Blair did not take the news about Jenny's friendship with Mainwaring very seriously. His prime suspect was Sandy Carmichael. He sent MacNab and Anderson up to the gallery to grill Jenny and then leaned forward and said threateningly, 'Carmichael is our man. Don't go digging up any mair suspects.'

'Meaning you want it to be Carmichael,' said Hamish cynically. 'A drunk can be shut up before he gets to court and starts talking about lobsters easier than anyone else. But you'll always have a problem. The press are getting tired of the witchcraft angle. They want to know about that skeleton and whose it was.'

'Bugger the press,' said Blair viciously. 'Why isnae there something to distract them? Why doesn't another Russian reactor blow? Why doesn't someone assassinate Maggie Thatcher?'

'If we could solve the witchcraft bit, they might begin to cool off,' said Hamish thoughtfully. 'That scaring o' Mrs Mainwaring, I'm sure it wasn't connected with the murder.'

'Then go and see what you can find out,' howled Blair.

Hamish was ambling down the main street in the direction of the manse when a voice behind him said 'Psst!'

He turned about and found himself looking down at Mrs MacNeil, she who had been so reluctant with directions when he first came to Cnothan.

'I know who murdered Mr Mainwaring,' she muttered.

'Tell me about it,' said Hamish.

She was carrying a heavy shopping bag. 'Look as if you've offered to carry this home for me,' she hissed.

Hamish looked at her curiously. The woman's eyes were glittering with excitement.

He took the bag from her and she led the way to the bungalow called Green Pastures.

The living-room of the bungalow was gloomy and dark and overfurnished. Victorian furniture designed for larger, grander rooms stood about looking as if it had been stored there before an auction. There were two black horsehair sofas, a Benares brass bowl full of dried pampas-grass, an enormous glass case that held a moth-eaten golden eagle, a carved oak sideboard like an altar, and black leather, horsehair-stuffed, high-backed chairs.

'Now,' said Mrs MacNeill, 'take out your notebook, Constable.'

Hamish dutifully produced pencil and note-book and waited patiently.

'It wass herself that did it,' said Mrs Mac-Neill triumphantly.

'Mrs Mainwaring?'

'Och, no. Mrs Struthers.'

'The minister's wife?' Hamish was tempted to put away his notebook. 'Why on earth would she do that?'

'It wass the microwave cooking class for the Mothers' Meeting,' said Mrs MacNeill eagerly. 'Herself wass giving the talk and very proud of herself and puffed up wi' vanity she was, too. Then Mr Mainwaring came in and he starts to criticize her and then he takes over the lecture himself. We all just went away, but I crept back after he had left, for herself said we could try the cooking and I saw no reason to waste money on my own dinner when I could eat some of the things she offered. She didnae see me, but I saw her. She was drinking sherry from the bottle, like a harlot.' Hamish blinked. 'And then she mutters something about killing Mr Mainwaring.'

Hamish's pencil stopped gliding over the pages of his notebook. An idea struck him. 'I'll just be off and have a word with Mrs Struthers.'

'You'll break the news gently to Mr Struthers,' said Mrs MacNeill eagerly. 'He's a fine man and he disnae ken he's married to an evil woman.'

'I won't be making any arrest yet,' said Hamish stonily. 'Thank you for the information.'

'A fine polisman you are,' said Mrs MacNeill waspishly. 'Mr MacGregor would have had her in the handcuffs.'

Hamish got to his feet. 'If ye can think o' anything else, Mrs MacNeill, let me know,' he said. And deaf to the complaints that followed him out of the house, he went on his way.

Mrs Struthers looked glad to see him. She fussed over him and gave him tea and scones. After they had exchanged some gossip, Hamish said, 'I have just been hearing about your lecture on microwave cookery.'

The minister's wife turned red. 'That was the most awful evening of my life,' she said. 'I could have killed that man.'

'But you didn't?'

Mrs Struthers sighed. 'I hadn't even the courage to stand up to him. I just stood there like a . . . like a . . . *humiliated rabbit!*'

'Aye, well, to get back to the original crime, the witchcraft scare. I was hoping your husband could help.'

'What on earth could he do? That's him coming now.'

'Och, I'll just have a wee word with him.'

* * *

That Sunday, Mr Struthers preached the most fiery sermon of his life. He claimed the three women who had frightened Mrs Mainwaring by pretending to be witches were as good as murderesses. They were murdering their own souls with malice and spite. With great relish, he outlined what would happen to them when they got to hell, and being jabbed by pitchforks was the least of what was waiting for them. He thundered and he blasted and he called down the wrath of God on Cnothan. He compared Cnothan to Sodom and Gomorrah. Unless the guilty confessed, there was no hope for them and no hope for Cnothan. Fire from Heaven would consume them all. The church was crowded. As Mr Struthers leaned over the pulpit, the congregation cringed back.

When Hamish left the church, he was surprised to see the sharp, foxy features of Detective Jimmy Anderson peering at him from the church porch.

'What are you doing here?' asked Hamish. He felt lightheaded from a long night on the moors searching for Sandy.

'Blair's idea,' said Anderson gloomily. 'Some woman called round at the hotel to make a statement that the minister's wife had done it. Blair tells me to go to church and clock the congregation. Seems Sandy Carmichael never missed a service. Blair didnae believe the woman's story but he gets this mad idea

135

that Carmichael might turn up. Any chance o' a dram?'

'I have some whisky at the police station,' said Hamish.

'Lead on, Macduff,' misquoted Anderson cheerfully. 'I need a good belt to get rid of the taste of all that hellfire and damnation.'

When they were seated in the police station on either side of the desk, Anderson asked curiously, 'I didnae know they still went in for sermons like that. No one's going to take it seriously, though.'

'You don't know Cnothan,' said Hamish. 'When approaching Cnothan, set your watch back one hundred years. It's a time warp here. Preach a sermon like that anywhere else in Sutherland – Lairg or Dornoch or Golspie – and the minister would soon find the worthies of the town petitioning for his transfer. For goodness' sakes, man, they still believe in fairies in this part o' the world.'

'Talking about fairies, one of the local louts is going around saying you're one yourself.'

'And which lout would that be?' asked Hamish curiously.

'A great big turnip heid called Alistair Gunn. Said you stank o' scent.'

'That wass my aftershave,' said Hamish stiffly. 'Or rather, it's MacGregor's. And if ye don't stop sniggering, I'll take that glass away from ye.'

Anderson changed tack. 'We didnae get much out o' that artist o' yours, Jenny Lovelace. Sticks to her story. Said he insulted her art. Said she was crying. Said she thought she'd sound daft if she told you what it was about, so she said her sister had died. She doesnae have a sister.'

'It's odd,' said Hamish. 'Her ex-husband in Canada did the same thing and she told me about that readily enough.'

'She's a grand painter,' said Anderson. 'My type of stuff. I cannae thole thae paintings o' people wi' two eyes on the one side of their head. Think she did it?'

'I don't know,' said Hamish. 'It takes a bit of strength and bottomless callousness to dump a full-grown man in a tank of lobsters.'

'He was dead at the time he hit the water,' said Anderson. 'The pathologist says as how someone struck him a blow on the back of the head which near broke his neck, so Mainwaring could've fallen over into the pool and the murderer could've run off and come back later to get rid o' the skeleton. Anyway, we know it's Sandy Carmichael. He probably got a fit o' the horrors and thought Mainwaring was a bunch o' green snakes.' He glanced up at the window. 'If I'm no' mistaken, here comes the village lout. Leave you to it.'

He scampered off just as Alistair Gunn came ambling in.

'Hoo are ye the day?' said Alistair with a great turnip grin and his eyes as hard as Scottish pebbles.

'Sit down,' said Hamish, eyeing him coldly. Alistair was wearing his usual hat, the leather one, peaked and shaped like an American baseball cap. He was wearing a game coat with rips in the sleeves, and his rubber boots exuded a strong smell of sheep dung.

'Now what do you want?' demanded Hamish.

'I've found your murderer for you,' said Alistair.

'That being?'

'Harry Mackay, the estate agent.'

'And why would Harry Mackay want to kill William Mainwaring?'

'Because Mainwaring was competing with him,' said Alistair triumphantly.

'Oh, aye, in what way?'

Alistair hitched his chair forward. 'Mainwaring bought thae cottages and crofts. Right? He got the land decrofted. He did it under false pretences. He disnae belong here. I put in ma objections to the Crofters Commission when I learned what was going on, but they told me the time for objections was long past.'

'I checked up on those houses,' said Hamish wearily. 'One had a damaged roof and the other had no bathroom and no electric light laid on. Mainwaring bought the one for ten thousand pounds and the other for eight. Small beer to a man like Mackay who sells castles.'

'You're all the same,' said Alistair bitterly. 'Mackay's a toff and ye willnae touch the toffs. It's one law for the rich and one for the poor.'

Hamish fought down his temper. He had heard Alistair trapped and shot game for sport, unlike most Highlanders, who only killed what they needed to eat. A brace of dead rabbits hung from his belt. He exuded a sort of peasant cruelty.

'I'll look into it,' said Hamish abruptly.

'Well, I'm sitting here until I get you to take down a statement,' said Alistair threateningly.

Hamish looked at him thoughtfully and then his thin face lit up in a charming smile.

'Stay as long as you like, you handsome brute, you,' he said softly.

Alistair Gunn stood up so quickly that the chair went flying.

'Oh, don't go,' cried Hamish. 'We have *lots* to talk about.'

The only answer was the slamming of the police-station door.

Hamish leaned back in his chair and clasped his hands behind his head and fought down the desire to go and see Jenny.

Any attraction she'd held for him had surely died when she had confessed to liking Mainwaring and to having lied about her sister. He had an uneasy feeling he had been allowed to share her bed to keep him quiet. And yet he wanted her. He wanted her very badly. Then he wanted a cigarette. Then the longing for her hit him in a second wave, more powerful than the first.

He was just convincing himself that it was all in the order of duty to ask her more questions when there was a commotion outside and then the doorbell rang.

Outside stood three couples, three schoolgirls, and the minister, Mr Struthers.

The minister herded the party into the police station as Hamish stood aside.

'Behold the guilty!' cried Mr Struthers, his pale eyes flashing with triumph.

Hamish collected chairs from the kitchen and waited until everyone was seated. Then he took out his notebook. He looked at the three schoolgirls, who were sitting with their heads hanging.

'I guess I am looking at the Mainwaring witches,' said Hamish. 'Names?'

Mr Struthers acted as spokesman. The girls were all fourteen years old. They were Alison Birrell, Desiree Watson, and Marleen Macdonald.

Hamish pricked up his ears at the sound of the names Birrell and MacDonald.

He interrupted Mr Struthers. 'Mr Birrell and Mr Macdonald – you are both crofters?'

140

Birrell was a tough little dwarf of a man and Macdonald an enormous giant. Both nodded.

Their wives were sitting holding hands and sobbing.

'And Mr Watson?'

Jimmy Watson, a dapper little man in a blue serge suit, said, 'Motor mechanic.'

Hamish looked at the minister. 'I think it would be better, Mr Struthers, if you took the parents through to the living-room and left me to have a word in private with the girls.' He saw the parents were about to protest and added quickly, 'I will not be taking statements until you are present.'

Reluctantly, they shuffled out.

'Now,' said Hamish, perching on the edge of his desk. 'We'll just have a wee talk.'

The girls all looked remarkably alike. Two had red hair and one black, but they had the same sullen, pinched white faces and beaky noses. Bad diet, thought Hamish. Boil-in-the-bag meals and fish and chips.

He selected the more composed-looking girl, Desiree Watson, and said, 'You, Desiree, what on earth were you thinking of to scare poor Mrs Mainwaring?'

'We couldnae get rid o' Mr Mainwaring,' sniffled Desiree, 'so we thought we could frighten his missus into getting him to leave.'

'But why should you three girls take it upon yourselves to do this?'

141

Alison Birrell spoke up. 'Will we go to the bad fire, mister?'

Hamish decided that if he reassured them on that point, he would not get another word out of them.

'If you do not make a full confession,' he said, 'I shudder to think what will happen.'

The girls clutched each other and began to cry again.

Hamish soothed them down. Haltingly, it all began to come out. They had heard their parents complaining and complaining about Mainwaring. Mainwaring had said that Mr Watson, the motor mechanic, had overcharged him and had reported the garage to the Consumers Council. So the girls had planned to take matters into their own hands. They had waited behind the churchyard wall until they heard Mrs Mainwaring coming along.

After half an hour of close questioning, Hamish called the minister and the parents back in and took statements from the girls.

'Will they go to prison?' asked Alec Birrell.

'Not if they co-operate,' said Hamish, thinking quickly. 'This witchcraft nonsense is stopping anyone from seeing the facts of the disappearance of William Mainwaring clearly.' He saw the freelance reporter, Ian Gibb, passing along the street outside and opened the door and called to him.

'Come along, Scoop Gibb.' Hamish grinned. 'Another exclusive for you.'

Blair was sitting in the television lounge of the Anstey Hotel, drinking beer, when Hamish reported to him.

'What?' roared Blair. 'You daft pillock. Didnae you charge them with something?'

'I did better than that,' said Hamish. He told Blair of giving the freelance reporter the story. 'Don't you see, man,' said Hamish, 'the sooner the press stop asking questions about witchcraft and that skeleton, the better? We're left with the skeleton, but at least this should take some of the heat off.'

'Damn waste o' time,' growled Blair. 'I can't move without tripping over television cables. With Mrs Mainwaring identifying these teeth and once the dentist in Edinburgh confirms it, the funeral will be held and that'll be more mayhem in the press.'

'Have you considered it's going to get out sooner or later?' said Hamish. 'The lobsters, I mean.'

'It can't get out,' said Blair. 'If it gets out I'll lose my job, and I'll make sure you lose yours too. Shuddup. Here's the news.'

He crouched forward, his hands clasped and his head bent in a ludicrous attitude of prayer.

The news started off with the headlines. A bomb had gone off in Number 10 Downing Street. Intended to kill the Prime Minister, it had not succeeded but had killed two members of the Cabinet, a policeman, two detectives, and a messenger. Hamish watched in a dazed way. The next headline was that the tail-end of the American hurricane Bertha had struck the Clyde estuary. Ships had gone down, people had been killed by flying slates, trees uprooted, and cars blown off bridges.

'Oh my God,' breathed Blair. 'Saved by the bell. Was ever a man so lucky!'

Thoroughly sickened, Hamish walked out. The hotel was a buzz of activity with reporters packing up and photographers paying bills; the air was full of the sound of cars revving up in the car park outside.

Chapter Seven

While Titian was grinding rose madder
His model was posed on a ladder,
Her position to Titian
Suggested coition
So he dashed up the ladder and had her.
– Anonymous

Hamish was standing in the forecourt of the hotel, moodily watching the hectic departure of the press. Ian Gibb was running frantically from one to the other, crying, 'You won't forget? You'll ask your editor?' Obviously he had been trying to wangle a job on some paper in the south.

'Macbeth!'

Hamish swung around and looked at Blair, who had followed him out, his eyes quite blank. Hamish was reflecting he had never before disliked the Detective Chief Inspector quite so much as he did at that moment.

'I want ya tae go doon tae Inverness the morrow,' said Blair, 'and check out Jamie Ross's alibi. The wedding was held at the Glen Abb Hotel on Ness Bank.'

'But the Inverness police have already checked it out,' said Hamish crossly. 'There was a point at the wedding reception when no one can quite remember seeing him, but he didn't have his car and he didn't take the train or bus.'

'Look, jist do as you are told, laddie. He was missing for a bit. See if anyone in Inverness saw him. And don't argue. And leave the Land Rover. You can take the morning train.'

Hamish opened his mouth to protest and then thought the better of it. He would be out of Cnothan and away from the town and its residents, and he might be able to think more clearly.

He nodded and turned away and walked up the village street.

Jimmy Anderson was waiting for him outside the police station. 'Any more whisky?' he asked hopefully.

'Aye,' said Hamish. 'But I would like ye to do something for me. Do it, and I'll get you a bottle o' the best malt.'

'Okay. What?'

'There's a Xerox machine at the hotel. Run me off a copy of all the statements and bring them along with you.'

146

'That'll take me ages,' grumbled Anderson.

'Come on,' said Hamish. 'No statements, no whisky.'

'I'll see,' said Anderson sulkily.

Hamish walked away, smiling. He knew Anderson would do almost anything for a free drink. He bought a bottle of whisky and went back to the police station.

Jenny was waiting for him outside. 'Any chance of a cup of coffee?' she asked.

She was wearing a dress, a soft red, clinging wool one, which moulded her figure. Her legs were not good, being much too plump and thick at the ankle. Hamish's eye ran over her, looking for other physical imperfections to cool his rising lust, but the general effect Jenny presented was one of warmth and prettiness.

As Hamish made the coffee, he told her about going to Inverness in the morning.

'Why?' asked Jenny. 'Surely that end has already been covered by the Inverness police.'

'I think Blair wants me out of the way,' said Hamish. 'He's anxious not to find the murderer.'

'Why on earth . . .?'

'Oh, he's an odd man,' said Hamish, remembering in time that he must not tell anyone about the lobsters.

'Can I come with you?' asked Jenny.

'No.'

'"No" meaning I am a suspect?'

Hamish tried to think of a gracious lie and failed. 'Yes,' he said.

'Do you think I did it?'

'I cannae say,' said Hamish miserably. 'I don't really know you.'

She stood on tiptoe and kissed the end of his nose. 'I thought you knew me pretty well.'

Hamish blushed and backed away.

'Oh, I see,' said Jenny. 'Not when you're on duty.'

'It's not that,' said Hamish. 'It's just I need to keep my mind clear.'

She edged her chair round the kitchen table until she was next to him. 'So I do disturb you,' she said. 'It wasn't just a one-night stand.'

'Of course not,' said Hamish uneasily. 'I am not in the habit of . . . I don't . . . I . . . I . . .'

'Don't what?' she giggled. 'You're blushing like a schoolgirl, Hamish.'

She stood up and went behind him and put her arms around his neck. He turned his head sharply around and pressed it into the softness of her breasts.

It was like being drunk, thought Hamish groggily an hour later.

They had been in the kitchen and next they were in his bedroom without their clothes on and he couldn't even remember having removed one stitch.

'You're a bad man, Hamish Macbeth,' he said aloud. Jenny let out a gentle snore. 'A bad man,' repeated Hamish. 'Are you going to ask her to marry you? You *should* ask her to marry you.'

The sharp ringing of the bell at the police-station end jerked him upright.

'Anderson!' cried Hamish, appalled. He shook Jenny awake. 'Jenny! Get up. It's that detective, Jimmy Anderson. He mustn't find you here.'

'Macbeth!'

The police station had not been locked and Anderson had walked in.

Jenny was struggling into her clothes at the same time as Hamish. He jerked open the bed-room window. 'Leave this way, Jenny,' he said urgently.

He picked her up and lifted her through the window. 'I'll look after Towser for you while you're away,' whispered Jenny. 'Bring him over tomorrow.'

'Right.'

'And give me a kiss.'

Hamish leaned through the window and kissed her.

'I've got the papers, Macbeth,' Anderson called. Jenny swung around in confusion. Not having found Hamish in the house, Anderson had decided to search the garden.

Jenny scampered off, not looking at the detective.

'She chust called around to say hello,' said Hamish. 'Go round to the police station.'

'Some hello.' Anderson grinned. 'Better fasten up your collar and cover that love bite.'

Hamish slammed the window shut.

When he got through to the police station, it was to find Anderson already seated at the desk with a sheaf of papers.

Hamish forgot his embarrassment, poured Anderson a drink, and then began to read the statements.

'Far be it from me to tell you how to do your job,' he murmured, 'but you don't seem to have been able to pin anyone down. Everyone in Cnothan seems to have been at The Clachan that Saturday night, but they can't remember when they arrived, who was there, or when they left.'

'Obstructive lot,' said Anderson.

'Oh, I'm with you there. But Blair usually gets you to bludgeon people so much they end up telling you something – anything concrete to get you off their backs.'

'Grand whisky this,' said Anderson.

Hamish looked at him sharply. 'In other words, you've all decided it would be better not to find the murderer.'

'I didnae say that,' said Anderson, holding his glass up to the light and squinting at it.

Hamish turned over the statements. 'Here! What was Mrs Struthers doing in The Clachan?'

'Oh, her. Collecting for famine relief in the Third World. Evidently she turns up with her tambourine on a Saturday night because she knows the drunks will hand over their money easily.'

Hamish moved on to Jenny's statement. He wondered that Blair had accepted it without comment. She had gone for a walk on Saturday morning with Mainwaring up to Clachan Mohr. They often went up there and took a flask of coffee. He had insulted her work. He had been laughing and smoking his pipe in between insulting her. She had smacked his face and knocked the pipe from his mouth. Then she had run away.

'I'm surprised Blair has such sensitivity towards the artistic soul,' said Hamish drily.

'Meaning what?' asked Anderson lazily.

'Meaning Jenny Lovelace and Mainwaring.'

'Och, all that stuff about artistic integrity and wounding her very soul? In Blair's opinion, she's a hot little baggage who was being screwed by Mainwaring and the affair turned sour.'

'Watch your mouth!' said Hamish furiously.

'Keep calm, friend. I'm not saying it. I'm only saying how Blair said it.' Anderson wondered whether to add that Blair had said that anyone who got into the sack with a daftie like Hamish Macbeth would open her legs for anyone, but decided against it.

Hamish fought down his anger. He was dismayed to realize he was furious because Blair's nasty comments held the ring of truth. Mainwaring had been nearly sixty and hardly an Adonis. But he had been a well-built man, and that marriage-of-true-minds bit might have been very seductive to a woman like Jenny.

The door of the police station opened and Diarmuid Sinclair walked in. Anderson gulped down the whisky in his glass and, picking up the bottle, walked off with it.

'You're really coming out of your shell,' said Hamish as the crofter sat down. 'Gadding about like a two-year-old. I'm off to Inverness in the morning, so if you want me to save you a trip, I'll buy that present for you. I've got to go to the Glen Abb Hotel to check Ross's alibi.'

'No,' said Diarmuid. 'I ha' a mind to go masel'. While you're there, book me a room at the Glen Abb, and see it has the telly and a private bathroom.'

'And dancing girls? You're living it up. What are you going to get young Sean?'

'A train set,' said Diarmuid dreamily, 'wi' wee houses and fields and tracks and all.'

'Set you back a bit,' said Hamish. 'Not to mention the price o' a room at the Glen Abb.'

'I've a good bittie put by,' said Diarmuid. 'You jist book me the room for Friday night.'

* * *

After the crofter had left, Hamish drove over to Mrs Mainwaring's and asked for a photograph of her husband. He had a vague notion of sending it down to London to Rory Grant on the *Daily Recorder*. The riots in Paris were over and the journalist might be able to find something out about Mainwaring from the newspaper files. He stayed as short a time as possible. The house and Mrs Mainwaring depressed him. Ashtrays were overflowing and dust had settled on everything, and Mrs Mainwaring had been well and truly drunk.

When he returned to the police station, he could see the lights shining from Jenny's cottage. He wanted her again. A cynical voice in his head told him he could if he wanted. His conscience fought it down. Hamish did not believe in love without responsibility. One more night in her arms and then he really would have to propose to her.

He settled down to read the Xeroxed papers thoroughly. Along with the statements, there were reports on Mainwaring's background from the police in the south. Mainwaring's brother, a lawyer, had said that Mainwaring had borrowed large sums of money from him over the years and had never paid them back. He had ended up refusing to see him or communicate with him. Mainwaring's two sisters said pretty much the same thing. Mainwaring's parents were dead. He had inherited a tidy sum from them when he was still a comparatively young man. He had bought an hotel in Devon, but had seemed to run it like a sort of 'Fawlty Towers', insulting the regular customers. Three years later, he had declared himself bankrupt.

Then came the surprise. Mainwaring had been married twice before. One wife, the daughter of a garage owner, had divorced him, and the other, an elderly lady, had died of a heart attack. A police comment said that Mainwaring had a reputation for having great success with the ladies.

Hamish fished out the photograph of William Mainwaring and looked at it. The small prissy features set in the large round head looked out at him. Amazing, thought Hamish. No accounting for taste.

As the small train chugged out of Cnothan next morning, Hamish settled back in his seat and felt himself begin to relax. Cnothan and all its dark hates and enmities and Bible-bashing religion was losing its grip on him and he was journeying towards the light. That's just what it was like, he thought. It was as if Cnothan was some science-fiction black mist that twisted and turned the minds of all who lived in it.

The train crawled its way round the hillsides, stopping and starting, finally picking up speed until at last it clattered over the points into Lairg station, the first civilized outpost in Hamish's mind. The sky was turning light and the birds were chirping in the trees. He leaned out of the window and watched the man in charge of Lairg station bustling about. Hamish knew him of old. He was like a station-master in a children's book, rosy-cheeked, white hair, kindly eyes twinkling behind spectacles, unfailingly helpful, unfailingly good-humoured.

Now Lairg, as Hamish remembered, was very like Cnothan in size and design. It, too, was the centre of a crofting community. But it was a bustling, cheerful, welcoming place.

The days were getting rapidly lighter. One long ray of sun struck the top of the station roof. There was a tinge of warmth in the air. That was the way of winter in the Highlands. It seduced you into thinking it had lost its grip and then came roaring back. The train moved off in a series of jerks, through Ardgay, Tain, Fearn, Invergordon, Dingwall, Muir of Ord, and on to Inverness.

The restless seagulls of Inverness were screaming overhead wĬhen he got off at Inverness station. The Tannoy was belting out a Scottish country-dance tune. Hamish was tempted to spend a day going around the shops, tempted to forget about the investigation. What on earth could he find out at this late date that the Inverness police could not? He was not wearing his uniform, correctly guessing that Blair had not warned the Inverness Police Department of this intrusion into their territory.

Inverness is the capital of the Highlands, crowded, busy, lively, and almost beautiful if you keep your eyes away from a big, grey, ugly modern concrete building that squats by the side of the River Ness and quite ruins the view of the castle.

It was past this architectural monstrosity that Hamish went, and then along Ness Bank to the Glen Abb Hotel.

The hotel had been created out of two large Victorian villas. The clever owner had kept the cosy Victorian effect with large overstuffed armchairs and log fires. The chef was French and the prices as high as those in a West End London restaurant, but the owner, Simon Gaunt, knew there was a lot of money in and around Inverness and not too much to spend it on in the way of entertainment.

He was in his office when Hamish arrived. He was a very thin, tall Englishman as gaunt as his name, wearing full Highland dress.

'The tourists like it,' he said, fidgeting with the hem of his kilt, although Hamish had made no comment.

Hamish explained that they were still trying to find out if Jamie Ross had been missing from the reception for enough length of time to get to Cnothan and back.

Simon Gaunt shook his head. 'Damn near impossible, I would say,' he said. 'The police have already asked me the same question and interviewed the waiters and other members of the staff. He went out for about an hour. Mr Ross said he had drunk too much and needed to clear his head. He said he walked up and down by the river for quite a while, until he felt sober enough to go back. But you know that. He evidently made a statement to that effect.'

Mr Gaunt poured himself a cup of coffee from a Thermos jug on his desk. Hamish sniffed the air and then looked at the hotel owner hopefully. The hotel owner stared back and put the top firmly back on the jug without offering Hamish any.

Hamish sighed inwardly. That's the English for you, he thought. He meant the southern English, the residents of Cumbria, Yorkshire, Lancashire, and Northumberland not really qualifying.

He fished in the pocket of his sports jacket for his notebook. He might as well take down some notes and type up a report for Blair to show he had been working. The photograph of William Mainwaring, which had been tucked between the pages of his notebook, fell out and slid over the desk to land in front of Mr Gaunt.

'Oh, are you after Mr Williams as well?' asked the manager, peering at the photograph.

'That's the dead man,' said Hamish sharply. 'William Mainwaring.'

Mr Gaunt fished in his sporran and brought out a pair of spectacles that he popped on his nose. He picked up the photograph again and then grinned. 'Well, I suppose Williams is better than Smith.'

'You mean Mainwaring was calling himself Williams? Not Smith? You mean he had a woman with him?'

'And what a woman,' said Mr Gaunt. 'I thought it was his daughter at first.'

Hamish thought of Jenny and his heart lurched.

'When was this?' he asked.

'About a month ago. They checked in for one night.'

'He was married,' said Hamish desperately. 'How do you know it wasn't Mrs Mainwaring?' – although Hamish knew that no one would ever describe Mrs Mainwaring as looking like her husband's daughter.

Simon Gaunt's face took on a dreamy look. 'She was like a Highland beauty dressed in Paris. Masses of shiny black hair falling to her shoulders, white skin, and the sort of mouth you dream about – full and sensual. She was wearing a cream wool dress with a white leather belt, black stockings, and scarlet high heels, those sandal-type with thin straps. They were in the dining-room for a long time. He was prosing on about something and she was looking at him with amusement, but she hardly said a word. I was in the dining-room myself that evening, for the Laird of Crochty was in. The laird likes to dine here.'

Hamish let out a little sigh of relief. Helen Ross. Not Jenny. He would worry about Helen Ross later, but right at that moment he was glad it hadn't been Jenny.

'Was that the only time they stayed here?' he asked.

'Yes, definitely. I wouldn't forget the likes of her in a hurry.'

Hamish asked more questions and then said, 'Oh, while I'm here, I would like to reserve one of your best rooms for Friday night for a Mr Diarmuid Sinclair.'

'And who's he?' asked the manager. 'I like to keep one of the best rooms free in case one of the laird's friends wants to stay overnight. The laird is very fond of my hotel.'

Hamish looked at the hotel owner in amazement. 'You mean to say you haff never heard of Mr Diarmuid Sinclair?'

'No, I can't say I have,' said Mr Gaunt.

Hamish laughed. 'He'll walk in here looking like an old crofter and sounding like an old crofter and no one would ever guess he made his millions as a young man in the South African gold mines.'

Mr Gaunt pretended to look carefully at the register. 'Why!' he said, 'we have our best suite free. It used to be a lounge but we turned it into our best suite with hall and bathroom. We have had royalty there.'

'Is that a fact,' said Hamish. 'Who?'

'When this was a private house, the queen paid a visit to Mrs Crummings, the then owner. Mrs Crummings was a retired house-keeper from Storroch Castle. The queen took tea in that very bedroom, although, of course, it was not a bedroom then.'

'My, my,' said Hamish. 'Queen Elizabeth herself.'

'Well, no,' said Mr Gaunt. 'Queen Mary.'

'I'm thinking that would be long before you were born,' said Hamish.

'Yes, yes,' said the hotel owner testily, 'but nonetheless, do assure Mr Sinclair that we have had royalty here.'

Hamish was escorted out of the hotel by Mr Gaunt, a friend of the famous Mr Diarmuid Sinclair meriting such distinguished attention. He walked along the river bank. He wondered whether he should warn Diarmuid that he had lied about him but decided against it. The sun was still sparkling on the water, but the wind had become chill and the sky was turning a murky colour.

He decided he would try to see Helen Ross alone before he said anything to Blair. Blair would not respect Jamie Ross's feelings but would accuse Helen in front of her husband of having spent the night with Mainwaring. Hamish sat down on a bench and stared at the water. Now that he was away from the atmosphere of Cnothan, strong motives for murder leapt into his mind. Jamie, for all his pleasant personality, was a hard-nosed businessman and probably had a ruthless streak. In order to succeed in the Highlands and cope with the hellish bureaucracy of crofting laws, landlords, factors, environmentalists, and God knows how many obstructive quangos, you had to be ruthless. And how would such a ruthless man take the infidelity of his wife? By ruining his business? Hamish shook his head, and a passing woman gave him a clear berth. Then there was Mrs Mainwaring. It was her money Mainwaring was using to wine and dine Helen Ross. Agatha Mainwaring was a powerful woman who drank too much. What if it was not a cold-blooded, premeditated crime, but done by someone who had found the incomer by the lobster tank, interfering as usual and poking his nose in where he had no right to be, and had struck him a blow that had broken his neck and toppled him into the tank? Maybe

161

whoever it was did not know Mainwaring was dead but thought that a few nibbles by the lobsters would serve him right, and had run away, only to return later to find Mainwaring had turned into a skeleton. Had the call that had sent him rushing off thirty miles to the Angler's Rest been made to keep him out of the way? Or had it been another practical joke to keep him from interfering with the locals' Saturday-night drinking pleasures? The witchcraft scare had not been connected to the murder. Or had it?

Land greed was a powerful force in the Highlands. The two crofters, Birrell and Macdonald, could have put their daughters up to the scare, roping in Watson's daughter as well in order to confuse the issue.

On the other hand, it could have been a practical joke that had gone wrong.

Say Alistair Gunn, not knowing his own strength, had pushed Mainwaring, and Mainwaring had struck his head on the side of the tank and broken his neck.

Or there was Harry Mackay. He had been grossly insulted by Mainwaring. 'Couldn't even get a fuck in a brothel,' or something like that, Mainwaring had said. Mackay had been furious. The insult to Mackay's masculinity might refer to something in the past. Had Mackay been married, engaged, and had Mainwaring with his uncanny way with women taken some female away from Mackay?

And Mrs Struthers? What of her? It was all very well to laugh at the idea that a minister's wife would turn to murder just because someone had humiliated her and jeered at her cooking skill. But Cnothan was such a dark and twisted sort of place, who knew what went on under the most respectable façade?

Hamish looked at his watch. There was a train due to leave at noon. He walked in the direction of the station. A poster caught his eye. There was a rerun of *Whiskey Galore* on at the cinema.

Damn Cnothan and damn Blair thought Hamish.

He headed rapidly in the direction of the cinema.

Ian Gibb went down to meet the evening train in the hope that Hamish might be on it. He was smarting with humiliation. The *Daily Recorder* in London had asked him for a story and he had duly sent one. It had appeared on the front page but under someone else's name. When he had phoned the news editor to complain, the news editor had pointed out that the reporter who had been blessed with a byline had deserved it, for he had had quite a job translating Ian's prose. Ian had hotly demanded an example. 'Well,' the news editor had said, 'take this line, for instance. "Said forty-eight-year-old electrician, Mr Joseph Noble, of 22 Main Street, Cnothan, yesterday laughingly, but with tears behind the laughter, 'This place will never be the same,'" For God's sake, sonny, you're not sending stuff to the local rag, you know.'

Ian had slammed down the phone. What had been up with that bit about Mr Noble? They hadn't even used it. He thirsted for another scoop . . . something that would make them sit up. Blair was hiding something. Forensic had been crawling all over Jamie Ross's place. Was that where Mainwaring had been last seen? But how had Mainwaring been reduced to a skeleton? And why did Blair get so red-faced and violent every time he asked if they had discovered the reason? Hamish might know.

Also, Ian smelled a cover-up somewhere. If it hadn't been for that bomb in Downing Street, the media would still be asking questions and more questions.

The train pulled in. Ian saw Hamish descending from a carriage at the end and ran to meet him.

'Not another murder?' asked Hamish.

'No, it's just that . . .' Ian launched into a long and bitter complaint against the *Daily Recorder* and the way one of the biggest murder mysteries of the century was being passed over.

Hamish thought hard as Ian talked. The lobster death could not be hushed up forever. Sharp interest would return and that interest would never fade. Television crews even a year later would return to do documentaries of what had happened to Mainwaring. So what if the upper class of London had a fright? It would make screaming headlines, but at least it might mean a murderer did not remain at large. If the press became pushy again, then Blair would be made to work.

'There is a story,' said Hamish cautiously, 'and you've just been talking about it.'

'What?' asked Ian eagerly.

'Well, the fact that this is a dreadful and grotesque murder and there's an uncanny silence about it. Blair sits around the Anstey Hotel watching television when he ought to be interviewing people again and again. Go round the locals and gossip to them and get them to voice outrage.'

A slow smile dawned on Ian's face. 'Thanks, Hamish. I'll start right away.'

'Another word of advice,' said Hamish. 'When you're writing for a paper like, say, the *Daily Recorder*, read a copy o' the damn thing first and carefully copy the style. It's no use writing a piece in the style of *The Scotsman*, say, when you want it in one of the tabloids. And it's no use writing a piece for the tabloids as if you are writing for a local paper. Have you got your car?'

'Yes,' said Ian, waving towards a hand-painted primrose-yellow Morris Minor with a 1950s licence plate.

'Then drop me off at Cnothan Game.'

Only half listening to the reporter as they drove along, Hamish tried to think of ways to get Helen Ross on her own. He knew his own liking and admiration of Jamie Ross were not allowing him to think clearly. But if there were more achievers like Jamie in the Highlands of Scotland, then the population figures might rise again. As it was, the young people drifted away to the cities, the houses and cottages stood empty, occasionally filled by an influx of underachievers who chattered on about the quality of life, by which they meant they could live on the dole while persuading themselves they were pioneers in the outback of the British Isles.

Ian dropped him in the yard of Cnothan Game and drove off. Hamish walked up to the door of the bungalow and rang the bell.

Helen Ross herself answered the door. She was wearing a black wool dress with enormous shoulder pads and jet-embroidered lapels, the sort of forties style worn by Joan Collins. Heavy antique earrings of Whitby jet emphasized the startling whiteness of her skin.

'Come in,' she said, and swayed off in front of him. He followed her into the sitting-room, automatically ducking his head as he walked under the chandelier.

'Jamie not at home?' asked Hamish.

'No, he's over on the west coast, seeing to the catch. Sit down. Would you like a drink?'

'Perhaps later,' Hamish sat down in one of the white leather armchairs and looked at Helen Ross curiously. She gave him a vaguely inquiring smile.

'I'm glad I found you alone,' said Hamish, and then he plunged right in. 'About a month ago, you and William Mainwaring booked into the Glen Abb Hotel in Inverness.'

Helen Ross lit a cigarette, blew out a cloud of smoke and squinted at Hamish through it.

'So you found out about that,' she said. It was not a question.

'Would you like to tell me about it?' Hamish waited while Helen placidly smoked. Her whole body appeared relaxed, and her long, long legs in the sheerest of black stockings were crossed at the ankle.

'Not really,' she sighed. 'But, if I have the right of it, it's either you or that pig Blair?'

Hamish nodded.

'Well, I'll tell you how it came about. I get pretty lonely here. Jamie's wrapped up in his work. I met him after I got my degree at St

Andrew's University. I was doing summer work, waitressing at the Anstey Hotel. We fell in love and got married and struggled along, being very happy just trying to make ends meet. Then Jamie thought up the idea for this business. It was very exciting. He worked at it night and day, like a man possessed. Then it succeeded, then we got rich, and then I got bored. End of story.'

The gentle, lilting Highland voice fell silent.

Hamish cleared his throat. 'So to relieve that boredom, you decided to have an affair with William Mainwaring?'

'No, it wasn't like that at all. He got in the way of calling around when Jamie was over at the west coast. He talked about books, paintings, world affairs, all the sort of things I used to talk about to my friends at university. He made me feel young again. Of course, it was all intellectual crap, now I come to think of it, but it was heady stuff. The conversation up here is about sheep, the weather, the church, and sheep. I was easily talked into going to Inverness with him. Jamie was to be away at the Land Court in Edinburgh, fighting another battle. William said we would stay at the Glen Abb – separate rooms – and have a slap-up meal and we could talk and talk. That was what was so seductive. Well, we were out of Cnothan and there we were in Inverness, and

William began to seem to me like a prosy bore who knew a little about everything and not much about anything. Then I found he had just booked the one room. I told him I was leaving. He said if I didn't spend the night with him, he would tell Jamie. So I said, "Tell Jamie," and I walked out in the middle of the night and found myself another hotel.'

'Which one?' asked Hamish.

'Not really a hotel, a boarding-house near the station, Mrs Parker's.'

'And what name did you check in under?'

'My own,' said Helen.

'And she will be able to vouch that you were there?'

'Of course she will. I was her only guest.'

'And did Mainwaring tell your husband about the trip to Inverness?'

'No.'

'How do you know?' asked Hamish curiously.

'Jamie's got a violent temper. He'd have broken Mainwaring's neck.'

'Then maybe he did.'

'He couldn't have,' said Helen, raising thin eyebrows in amazement. 'He was in Inverness with me at the wedding.'

'All the time?'

'No, he disappeared for a long time to sober up, but not long enough to get to Cnothan and back.'

169

'Is he often drunk?'

'He gets drunk on Hogmanay and then maybe occasionally at a party. The rest of the time, he hardly drinks at all. He likes coffee more than anything.'

Hamish sat in silence, thinking. Helen Ross went to the drinks trolley and mixed herself a gin and tonic. 'Sure you won't have anything, Constable?'

'No, thank you. What are you going to do now? asked Hamish. 'I'll need to put a report in to Blair. I can't keep this quiet.'

'I suppose you must,' said Helen. She sat down and crossed her legs. Her skirt, Hamish realized for the first time, was slit up the side and now exposed an expanse of long smooth stocking-leg and black stocking-top. Hamish wondered whether the leg show was deliberate. He could not imagine Helen Ross not being aware at any time of one inch of her body or dress.

'How will Jamie react?'

'I'll have to tell Jamie first. It might not be a bad thing. He'll learn what boredom can drive me to do. I've begged him to let me get a job, but he says the locals would sneer at him and say he's such a miser that he has to send his wife out to work.'

'I didn't think he would care what they thought.'

'Not in general. But he likes me here in the house, waiting for him. He'll be in such a rage. How boring.'

'He won't hurt you?' asked Hamish anxiously.

'Spoil the decoration he's paid so much for?' Helen laughed. 'I'm part of the show, along with those ghastly white leather chairs and the white Mercedes.'

'How do you mean, paid so much for?' asked Hamish sharply.

'The clothes, man, the clothes. This little number cost five hundred pounds and it's only one of many. My only enjoyment in life is buying clothes, and Jamie gladly pays for anything I want. He gives me everything except sex and company.'

Hamish shifted uncomfortably. The room was suffocatingly hot and suddenly charged with a new atmosphere. His collar felt tight and his skin itched.

He rose to go. Helen Ross rose as well and came to stand in front of him. In her high heels, she was as tall as he.

'Stay a little and have a drink,' she murmured. One hand with its long red-painted fingernails held the skirt of her dress open, her eyes dropping so that Hamish looked down as well.

'No, I have to be going,' said Hamish. His voice sounded strange in his own ears, all squeaky and afraid. She wound her arms round his neck and kissed him on the mouth. Hamish's senses reeled. Before Jenny had come on the scene, he had been celibate for a long time. Now he dimly wondered how he had ever managed to survive.

Helen's mouth had moved to his ear and she started nibbling the lobe. Her voice then whispered, 'Me going to Inverness with William has nothing to do with the case. You'll forget about it. Won't you?'

Hamish pushed her away and straightened his tie. 'No, Mrs Ross,' he said. 'I would like to help you, but I must put in my report.'

For one moment a flicker of . . . venom? . . . flashed in the depths of her eyes, and then it was gone.

When Hamish got outside a moment later, he gulped down great lungfuls of cold air. He set out to walk back to Cnothan.

Jamie Ross arrived home an hour later.

Helen Ross poured him a drink and then said, 'Hamish Macbeth was here. He has found out about me going to Inverness with Mainwaring.'

Jamie's face darkened. 'Is he going to put in a report?'

Helen shrugged. 'He says he'll have to.'

Jamie rounded on her. 'Didn't you try to shut him up, for Christ's sake?'

'Oh, I tried,' said Helen. 'Believe me, I tried. But he wasn't buying any.'

'Damn Macbeth to hell,' said Jamie Ross.

Chapter Eight

Loaf, as I have loafed aforetime,
Through the streets with tranquil mind,
And a long-backed fancy-mongrel
Trailing casually behind.
                    – S. Calverley

Hamish awoke the next morning in his own bed with Towser beside him. 'Anything would be better than you,' he said morosely, pushing the dog out of the bed. Towser usually lay across his master's feet like a rug during the night, but had been recently banished from the bedroom.

Hamish could have stayed the night with Jenny if he had wanted, but he had made the excuse that he would have to sit up late, typing out a report for Blair. Although this was true, he also did not want to get further involved until he decided whether his intentions were honourable or not.

The weather forecast for the north of Scotland had been dreadful, but as if to prove the forecasters wrong, the sun blazed down outside.

An hour later Hamish was about to descend on Blair with his report when the minister, Mr Struthers, called.

At first Hamish was puzzled. Why should a minister call on a policeman at breakfast time to discuss the problem of AIDS? Hamish grew more uncomfortable as the minister's pale eyes began to gleam with a hectic light as he went on to damn homosexuals. ' "Revenge is mine, saith the Lord," ' ended Mr Struthers.

'And a good thing too,' said Hamish cheerfully, trying to lighten the atmosphere. 'Revenge is best left to God and justice. Look at this murder. That came about because someone decided to take the law into their own hands.'

Mr Struthers leaned across the desk and seized Hamish's wrist in a strong clasp and his eyes bored into those of the policeman. 'Homosexuality is a form of murder,' he said.

Hamish picked up the minister's hand and removed it. The light began to dawn. 'It's a pity,' said Hamish, 'that you have not got the real-live homosexual in Cnothan to practise your lack of Christian compassion on. You're a terrible man for the gossip, Mr Struthers.'

'I never listen to gossip,' said the minister.

Hamish eyed him shrewdly. 'And so this wee visit has nothing at all to do with Alistair Gunn believing me to be gay?'

The minister flushed angrily. 'A certain parishioner came to me in great distress. He did not want to see AIDS in Cnothan.'

Hamish looked at the minister in disgust. 'You should be ashamed of yourself, Mr Struthers, listening to rubbish from that malicious man.'

'If I am mistaken, then I apologize,' said the minister. 'But where I find evil in my parish, I shall strike it down.'

'Would you say William Mainwaring was evil?' asked Hamish curiously.

The minister shifted uneasily. 'He has suffered the wrath of God.'

'Mainwaring suffered at the hands of a very evil human being, and if you want to spend your time striking out evil in your parish, then it is better you look for the murderer,' said Hamish furiously. 'Push off, there's a good minister, and close the door behind you.'

'Daft,' muttered Hamish after the minister left. 'They're all plain daft.'

He walked down the main street in the sunshine, wishing it were all over, wishing the murder solved and himself back in Lochdubh.

He met Diarmuid Sinclair and told him about the room having been booked for him at the Glen Abb Hotel, and continued on down the hill. A car slowed to a halt beside him, and Harry Mackay, the estate agent popped his head out.

'Like to come back to the office with me for a coffee?' he called.

Hamish hesitated only a minute. Blair could wait. Harry Mackay might throw some light on the mystery.

The estate office was in a Victorian villa in the middle of the council houses. The office was in what used to be the front and back parlours on the ground floor. Harry Mackay led the way upstairs to his living-room, which was above the shop.

When he went off to make coffee, Hamish studied the bookshelves.

He turned round as the estate agent came back in carrying a tray with coffee and biscuits.

'This is very kind of you,' said Hamish.

Harry Mackay grinned. 'I'm hoping to find out how our murder's going. Blair won't tell anyone anything.'

'It's not going anywhere,' said Hamish gloomily. 'Sandy Carmichael is the prime suspect and he hasn't been found.' Hamish then sat still, the coffee-cup half raised to his lips and his mouth open. He remembered sitting by the river in Inverness, thinking about all the suspects, and yet he had never once thought of Sandy Carmichael. Why? Surely it followed that the nosy Mainwaring had called round to bait Sandy and Sandy had struck him and shoved him in the pool. The very fact that Blair kept insisting it was Sandy had made him, Hamish Macbeth, discount the whole idea. There was the question of the clothes. Someone had got rid of the clothes. Surely the lobsters hadn't eaten clothes, wallet, credit cards, watch, and all the other indestructible bits without leaving a trace. Teams of policemen had combed the area for miles around, looking for any sort of fragment, and they hadn't come up with so much as a button. But there were peatbogs where a parcel of clothes would sink without a trace. Sandy's cottage had been gone over. There had been evidence in the garden at the back that a fire had recently been lit, but there had been no ash to sift through. The Land Rover had been scrubbed and hosed down. When had Sandy ever bothered to clean his Land Rover before?

Hamish felt like a fool.

'What's the matter?' asked Harry Mackay. 'You look as if you've just been struck by lightning.'

'Nothing,' mumbled Hamish. He pulled himself together. 'How's business?'

'Not very good. There's only one strange thing, Mrs Mainwaring called to see me. As soon as all the legal formalities are over, she wants me to buy the crofts and houses. I have a client for them in Edinburgh. Interested in holiday homes.'

Hamish's eyes sharpened. 'But not her own? She'll be staying on there?'

'Yes, her own as well. I warned her I can't get her much. I may get six thousand pounds apiece for the crofts if I'm lucky, but the houses are in a worse state than when Mainwaring bought them.'

'But Mrs Mainwaring has always said she liked Cnothan.'

'Well, she told me she'll be glad to get out. Wants to go back and live in Maidstone. And I'll tell you another thing: she was stone-cold sober. I used to wonder how on earth she put up with Mainwaring, but she told me he held the purse-strings and if she had left him, she wouldn't have got anything.'

'He had a rare way with the ladies, I gather,' said Hamish.

'Not that I ever noticed,' said Harry Mackay.

'Didn't interfere in your love life?' asked Hamish.

'What love life?' countered Harry Mackay. 'There's only two lookers around here. One's that artist and the other's Helen Ross.'

'And no success there?'

'No. I took Jenny Lovelace out for dinner a couple of times, but no go, and Helen Ross's come-hither eye doesn't mean a thing.'

'Who do you think did it?' asked Hamish. 'The murder, I mean.'

'Oh, don't ask me. This place is getting me down. They're all sick and twisted and narrow-minded and malicious.'

'I thought you were a Cnothan man yourself?'

'Aye, but I've been away from it for a long time, and I haven't been able to settle since I came back.'

Hamish took his leave and went to the Anstey Hotel, where he found Blair half asleep in the television lounge. A children's show flickered on the screen.

'Do you usually watch "Postman Pat"?' asked Hamish.

Blair came fully awake with a grunt. 'I was thinking about clues,' he said huffily. 'Got something for me?'

Hamish sat down and began to read his report on Helen Ross.

'Fancy whore,' said Blair when Hamish had finished. 'Ah'll go and see her maself and have some fun.'

'Don't have too much fun,' warned Hamish, 'or Jamie'll have his lawyer breathing down your neck.'

'Get oot o' here,' snarled Blair, 'and don't tell me what tae do. Bugger off.'

Hamish went off out into the soft sunlight. It was a mellow day, too good a day for one constable to be fuming over a pill of a detective inspector.

All at once, he decided to go fishing. He had a telescopic rod in his luggage. He would go to the upper reaches of the Cnothan River and if the water bailiffs caught him, he could swear blind he was looking for clues. He needed peace and quiet to think.

He kept on his uniform – proof to any water bailiffs that he was on duty – and ambled over with Towser loping at his heels. He had strapped the collapsible rod on to his back under his waterproof cape.

As he strolled along beside the foaming river, he wished he had not worn his cape. The sun was quite warm, although clouds were massing to the west and the wind was becoming chill.

It struck him that he had not thought of Priscilla for some time and he wondered whether he was cured.

Priscilla Halburton-Smythe sat in a chair in the hat shop in the King's Road and searched the newspapers for some mention of Cnothan. But the papers were still full of the aftermath of the Downing Street bombing.

The shop door opened and her friend, Sara Paterson, who owned the shop and shared a flat with Priscilla, came in. Priscilla's eyes slid to the clock. Eleven in the morning! Sarah was always late.

'I brought you a letter,' said Sarah. 'Arrived after you left.'

Priscilla took the letter and opened it. It was from her father. Her eye skimmed down it, looking for some mention of Hamish. Ah, here it was. Colonel Halburton-Smythe was incensed that Hamish Macbeth was still absent from Lochdubh. He had written to the Chief Constable to complain. It was an insult, leaving Lochdubh without a policeman, even though Hamish Macbeth was a gangling, useless lout. Priscilla's father thought his daughter was too friendly with the village policeman and never missed an opportunity to malign Hamish.

It dawned on Priscilla all at once that London was a very boring place compared to the Highlands of Scotland. 'Nothing ever happens here,' she said aloud.

'Oh, but darling, it *does*!' trilled Sarah. 'I met Peter Twist at a divine party last night and he's going to buy this white elephant of a shop from me.'

'You might have warned me you were thinking of selling,' said Priscilla angrily.

'Don't be cross, sweetie. You won't be out of a job. He's going to have all these divine fashions. All black leather, you know. The shop's going to be called Champers Campers and we're to stand around in his creations.'

'I don't think so, Sarah darling,' said Priscilla. 'I'm getting out. I mean I'm going north.'

'What? Leave London for the sticks just when everything's happening? I know what it is – you've got a fellow tucked away up there.'

'Don't be silly,' said Priscilla coolly. 'Look, there's two women about to come in. Let's see if we can sell something for a change.'

Hamish trudged on, looking for a quiet reach or pool where he could fish without being accused of poaching. The path now ran parallel to the river, but high above it. Then he saw, below him, a quiet pool surrounded by tangled undergrowth. He could sit quietly and fish and he would be able to hear any water bailiff approaching since the spot could be reached only with difficulty.

He slipped and scrambled down, with Towser slipping and scrambling down behind him.

Hamish unstrapped his rod and began to put it together. It didn't seem such a good idea now as it had seemed earlier when the sun had been shining. It was now bitter cold, the sky was changing from light grey to dark grey, and the wind scudded across the black surface of the water.

Towser, who always seemed impervious to the cold, sat down beside his master and watched the water.

Then the dog began to shift uneasily. It let out a faint whimper, sniffed the air, and pawed at Hamish's arm. Hamish stiffened and sniffed the air too. The wind had shifted from the west to the north-west and on it came the sickly sweet smell of decomposing corpse.

Hamish got to his feet. 'Fetch,' he said to Towser, but the dog backed away, whimpering dismally.

Hamish felt a sick lurch in his stomach. If the smell had come from a rotting animal carcass, then Towser would not have been upset.

He wedged his rod between two rocks and, still sniffing the air, he began to search around. Up to the left of where he had scrambled down, the smell grew stronger. Diligently sniffing, pausing, and sniffing again, Hamish got down on his hands and knees and crawled through the close-packed undergrowth of fern and bramble and gorse.

He stopped and crouched still. The smell was now so strong it made him want to retch. And then he saw it.

A pale hand was stretching out from under a bush.

Hamish lay on his stomach and looked under the bush and the dead eyes of Sandy Carmichael stared back.

He ran back to the pool and grabbed his fishing rod and collapsed it and fled up the hill with Towser at his heels.

Blair, Anderson, and MacNab arrived just as the blizzard struck. With Hamish, they huddled under the bushes by the rotting corpse waiting for reinforcements. At one moment, it seemed as if they would never come, and then they were all there, glaring lamps lighting up the dreadful scene as a tent was erected over the bush and body. Then came the pathologist, who was hailed with relief by Blair.

'Ye'll find it a clear case o' death from exposure,' said Blair. 'He was on the run, drunk, crawled under that bush, and never woke up. Ah, well, that wraps up the case.' Blair pulled a flask from his pocket and took a stiff drink. He winked at Hamish. 'Nae problem about lobsters now, lad,' he said. 'The murderer's dead and we can say what we like.'

Hamish said nothing, but watched as the pathologist crept into the tent.

After what seemed a very long time, he backed out.

'Well?' demanded Blair eagerly.

'A clear case of murder,' said the pathologist. 'Struck a heavy blow on the back of the head.'

'Couldnae he hae done it hisself?' pleaded Blair.

'Of course not,' snapped the pathologist. 'I shall be phoning my report to the procurator fiscal. Get photographs quick or we'll all be snowed in.'

Hamish shovelled a path to the foot of the drive the next day. He had just reached the gate when a snowplough passed and blocked him in again, throwing up a huge wall of snow against the front gate. By the time he had cleared it, he felt sweaty and gritty. He went indoors, had a shower, changed into his uniform, and went down to the Anstey Hotel.

The blizzard, luckily for Blair, had kept most of the press away, but Hamish arrived just in time to hear Ian Gibb asking, 'Who found the body?' and Blair's reply of 'Some local idiot.'

Hamish felt too angry to stay. Blair would withhold all information possible from him. He bumped into Jimmy Anderson outside the hotel. 'I'm frightened to go in there,' said Anderson with a grin. 'Blair's roaring mad. His chief suspect murdered.'

'Definitely murdered?'

'Oh, yes. And another thing: he had a hundred pounds on him.'

'It couldnae ha' been his savings,' said Hamish. 'A drunk like Sandy wouldn't have been able to keep a penny.'

'Aye, and he must have been trying to blackmail the murderer. A hundred pounds would have kept his mouth shut.'

'Until the next time he was drunk,' said Hamish sadly. 'It's no wonder he was killed.'

Anderson went into the hotel and Hamish walked down to the waterfront. The snow was thinning and he could see the other side of the loch. An army rescue helicopter stood on a flat piece of ground by the jetty, the pilot standing outside it, smoking.

Hamish ambled up to the pilot. 'You aren't dropping emergency supplies yet?' he asked.

The pilot shook his head. 'There's more bad weather coming. I'm just about to go up to pick out the houses that'll need it most and make sure there's no one in difficulties.'

A pale ray of sunlight struck the loch. 'Are you going up right now?' asked Hamish.

The pilot stubbed out his cigarette. 'Aye, I'm on my way.'

'Any chance of coming along for the ride?' asked Hamish, who had a sudden longing to soar high above Cnothan and everyone and everything in it.

'Sure, hop in.'

Hamish felt his spirits lifting as the helicopter started to rise. The clouds were rapidly thinning. He sat very still, with his hands on his knees, like a child on a fairground ride, staring down at the Christmas-card countryside with delight. The pilot began to ask questions about the murder, and Hamish answered absentmindedly, his eyes on the white scene spread out below.

'Needn't bother about those two cottages,' said the pilot. 'They're empty.'

Hamish could see the two houses far below and then beyond them, towards Cnothan, Mrs Mainwaring's bungalow. He could see Mrs Mainwaring herself, shovelling snow.

'Would you believe it,' said the pilot. 'There's the train. I wouldn't have thought it would have got through. They must have had a plough out on the line early this morning.'

The helicopter banked. The railway line curving out of Cnothan disappeared into the hills in a fantastic loop. In the days when it had been built, it had meandered all over Sutherland to take in the country homes and shooting lodges of the rich. Then the whole scene was blotted out as the sun disappeared and the blizzard came roaring back.

Like most people in Sutherland, Hamish had not bothered to lock the door when he had left. As he trudged up to the police-station drive, which was already becoming thickly covered with snow again, he could hear voices from the kitchen.

He opened the door. Diarmuid Sinclair and Jenny were sitting drinking coffee. A huge box stood on the floor.

'Oh, Hamish,' said Jenny, 'you must help. Mr Sinclair's bought a train set for young Sean and he wants you to put it together first to see if it works. He can't understand the instructions and I'm no good at that sort of thing either.'

'I shouldnae be wasting time,' said Hamish guiltily. 'There's been another murder.'

'We know. That Mrs MacNeill just called to find out why you hadn't arrested herself. I asked who herself was but she wouldn't tell me.'

'She thinks the minister's wife did it,' said Hamish, kneeling down on the floor and beginning to open the box.

'Of course she would,' said Jenny. 'She's got a crush on Mr Struthers. Even when her husband was alive – and that was only four years ago – she was chasing the minister. This is becoming really scary. Whoever murdered Sandy and William must be a maniac.'

Hamish thought he would just assemble a few bits and then leave them to do the rest. He was a policeman and however obstructive his superior officer might be, he, Hamish Macbeth, should be on the job.

But it was soothing, fascinating work as the miniature landscape grew under his fingers with its tiny trees and little stations.

Finally the toy railway was complete. Jenny and Diarmuid sat on the floor and watched enraptured as the trains whizzed around and around.

Hamish stood up. 'I'll make us all some more coffee and then I'll be on my way.'

He smiled indulgently down at Jenny and Diarmuid, who were as excited as children. And then he stared down at the miniature landscape, the coffee-pot in one hand, his mouth hanging foolishly open.

He rushed to the kitchen cupboard and took out a packet of soap powder and ripped open the top and then let the soap granules drift down on to the toy railway landscape like snow.

'Here, ye daft gowk!' roared Diarmuid. 'Whit dae ye think ye're daein'?'

'Stop it, Hamish!' screamed Jenny. 'You're ruining Diarmuid's present.'

Hamish dropped the soap packet and pulled on his oilskin cape. 'Tell Blair I'll be away for a wee while,' he said.

Diarmuid and Jenny stared at each other in amazement as Hamish hurtled out of the kitchen door. The Land Rover had been returned by Anderson. They heard a roar as it started up and skidded off down the drive.

'Don't worry, Mr Sinclair,' said Jenny. 'I'll get the vacuum and take the top off and get all that soap up. I'm not telling Blair anything. He'll just roar at me and say Hamish is mad and I won't be able to disagree with him!'

The train that had brought Diarmuid Sinclair back to Cnothan had also brought the day's supply of papers. Perhaps because he had not had time to think up any choice nuggets of flowery prose, Ian Gibb had jumped from amateur reporter to professional in one bound. The *Daily Recorder* carried the story of the new murder on the front page and a feature by Ian, headlined HIGHLAND POLICE COVER-UP? in the inside centre pages.

Blair's fury now knew no bounds. He received several very nasty phone calls from his superiors. He had tried to get the pathologist to lie and say that Sandy's murder had been suicide and the pathologist had duly reported this in his report.

The Detective Chief Inspector saw his job at risk. He went to the police station to take his fright and temper out on Hamish Macbeth and nearly had a fit when he found no Hamish but a crofter and that artist, playing with toy trains on the kitchen floor.

As the day wore on and there was no sign of Hamish, Blair sat down to compose a report.

If he got any satisfaction out of this mess, it would be the satisfaction of getting Hamish Macbeth fired.

Two days went by. The blizzard was over and the roads were clear and the press were gathering like vultures. Blair's Chief Superintendent in Strathbane had read his report on the iniquities of Hamish Macbeth, had asked a colleague what it was all about, and the colleague had said laconically that the village copper was rumoured to be the one who had solved two previous murders in Sutherland although Blair had taken the credit, and so Blair's report was probably spite.

The Chief Superintendent had phoned Blair and had told him acidly not to waste time writing stupid nonsense about a local bobby but to get on with solving the crime. 'What about the lobsters?' Blair had wailed. He was told that the matter of the lobsters would be coped with when and if Blair got his murderer.

He tossed and turned all night. Hamish had not run off for fun, he decided. Hamish Macbeth had found an important clue and wasn't sharing it. If he solved this crime, there would be no chance of Blair's getting the credit. Hamish had had a taste of filling a police sergeant's boots. He had probably become power-mad. Not, thought Blair, as the pale dawn crept into the hotel bedroom, that Hamish had shown any great flair for detective work in the past. It had been all luck. In each case, Hamish had all the suspects together and had confronted them and the guilty one had cracked.

Blair sat up suddenly. That was it! He would round up everyone he could think of who might have had a grudge against Mainwaring and hold a meeting in The Clachan. He would keep them there and sweat them for as long as the law allowed until something gave.

He picked a half bottle of whisky up from the bedside table and drank a hearty swallow. As the spirit shot from his stomach to his brain, he became more convinced that his plan would work.

When Hamish Macbeth came gangling back, he would find the case solved.

Chapter Nine

Truth will come to light; murder cannot be hid long.
> – William Shakespeare

They had all been cooped up together in The Clachan, on and off for two days now. Tempers were wearing thin, and several of the people present now had their lawyers in attendance.

It was this communal, brutal interrogation that was infuriating them all. Jenny's walks with Mainwaring and his criticism of her painting were out in the open, as was Helen Ross's visit to Inverness. Jamie Ross tried to punch Blair and was held back by his lawyer. The lawyer explained that Mrs Ross had never intended to have an affair with Mainwaring but had gone with him, with her husband's full knowledge, to find out what he was up to. Mr Ross had suspected Mainwaring of being about to start up a rival business.

Jenny was then accused of having an affair with Mainwaring. When she hotly protested, she was told bluntly that as she was sleeping with the local bobby, it followed her morals were questionable. Jenny promptly crossed the room and hired the services of the Rosses' lawyer, and Blair glared at her in baffled fury.

He was just getting his teeth into Agatha Mainwaring again when the door of The Clachan swung open and Hamish Macbeth strode in. He tugged off his oilskin cape and looked sadly around the assembled group. Mrs Struthers was crying quietly and her husband was comforting her. Helen Ross had lost all her usual poise and was lighting one cigarette from the butt of another. Hamish could smell Alistair Gunn's fear from across the room. Davey Macdonald, Alec Birrell, and the mechanic, Jimmy Watson, were all there with their wives and daughters. Mrs MacNeill was there, too. Harry Mackay was sitting next to the Rosses, almost hidden behind a cloud of blue cigarette smoke. All eyes turned in Hamish's direction.

'You can all go home,' said Hamish Macbeth wearily. 'Except for Harry Mackay. He's the murderer.'

There was a terrific uproar. Ignoring Blair's blustering and roaring, Hamish Macbeth walked across the room and stood over the estate agent. In a clear voice he charged him

Dornoch Firth railbridge idea was scrapped, the government still wanted to show they weren't neglecting Scotland and so they'd decided on a cheaper compromise, that of cutting off that great loop before it gets to Cnothan and replacing it with a straight line of track. That track would go right through Mainwaring's three crofts. Now, the compensation that would be paid for the loss of crofting land would be immense. I noticed when I was flying over Cnothan that the geographical lie of the land along through Mainwaring's crofts would make an ideal railroad track. I went to the police and found Mr Anstruther was part owner of a gambling club. I visited the club, and by bribing one of the staff to look at the books, I found that Harry Mackay owed Anstruther a considerable amount of money.

'When Anstruther learned he might be involved in a murder case, he caved in. The deal would have gone through the estate agent's books in the normal way. When Anstruther got the compensation from the government, he would wipe out Mackay's debt and still have a fortune. It is my belief that if Mackay had not moved to wipe out that debt, then Anstruther would have had *him* wiped out. The police tell me there's been bad stories about the ways he copes with people who don't pay up. Anstruther was brought up on the croft next to Mainwaring's. He felt that

Mainwaring must have known about the railway and had conned his relatives into selling the croft cheap. Anstruther planned to set up as a crofter until the compensation came through. As the son of a crofter and having been brought up on the croft, he would have no difficulty with the Crofters Commission.

'When I was in your house a few days ago, Mackay,' said Hamish. 'I noticed you had a lot of books on your shelf on alcoholism. You knew if you left that drink for Sandy Carmichael on the lobster tank that he would drink it and then want more. That would get him out of the way. You phoned me and got me to drive out to the Angler's Rest. You knew Mainwaring had advised Ross not to employ Sandy and would come around, poking his nose in, sooner or later. Mind you, it was a gamble, but then you *are* a gambler.'

Harry Mackay found his voice. It came out as a croak. He cleared his throat and said, 'It's all a load of rubbish, Macbeth. Okay, so I owed Anstruther money, but he's your man. He had every reason to hate Mainwaring. He knew Mainwaring had pulled a fast one. And those books on alcoholism were for my sister. She was down in Inverness in the alcoholic unit and I sent away for them, but by the time I got them, she had disappeared.' His lips trembled and he took out a handkerchief and wiped his mouth.

'I had nothing to do with it. Nothing. And you can't prove it.'

Hamish kept his eyes fixed on Mackay. 'Two deaths,' he said in a gentle, lilting voice. 'Sandy knew what you'd done and so you killed him. Two deaths, and all for nothing. But there's one thing you didn't tell your friend Anstruther, and that was that the whole railway project was scrapped a month ago, and if he found you had bought him three worthless properties ... We don't have the death penalty – yet – but Anstruther would have been glad in that case to act as our executioner. He may very well yet, for I had great pleasure in telling him about the collapse of the scheme. The bailie he had bribed to give him information from the first secret meeting about the railway had resigned by the time of the second secret meeting, which cancelled the project.

'So what's it to be, Mackay? A nice safe police cell or Anstruther's boys after you?'

There was a long silence. No one spoke, no one moved. The rising wind moaned around The Clachan and snow pattered on the window panes.

'It wasn't planned,' said Mackay in a tired voice. 'I followed him. He was going to report me to my head office. They would have fired me. I daren't lose my job. I didn't think Mainwaring really knew about the railway project. I thought he was just buying up cheap

200

property in the hope it would rise in value one day. He never had a good head for business.

'He insulted me in The Clachan. I left and then waited for him to leave. I followed him to Cnothan Game. I found a bit of rusty pipe by the road and put it in my pocket. But, man, man, I still didn't mean to kill him. He poked around and tried the office door but it was locked. I followed him into the lobster shed. He sat on the edge of the main tank and took out a notebook and began to write. There was an empty glass by the side of the tank. He put the note down by the tank. I knew it was a note for Jamie saying something about Sandy abandoning his post. Mainwaring never thought Sandy would return. All my hatred for the man boiled up in me and at the same time I realized in a flash that with him gone, Mrs Mainwaring might sell and then I would be safe from Anstruther. I struck him hard, and he fell into . . .'

But Blair moved like lightning. He thrust Hamish aside and clapped a large beefy hand over Harry Mackay's mouth.

'Enough o' this,' he shouted. 'Anderson! MacNab! Take him off tae Strathbane and book him.'

'And so,' said Hamish Macbeth that evening to Jenny Lovelace, 'I don't know why Blair

201

shut him up at that point.' But Hamish did know. Blair had seen the bit about the lobsters coming up.

Hamish wondered how on earth Blair would suppress the evidence.

Jenny looked at his drawn face and said quietly, 'Want to be left alone tonight?'

Hamish most definitely did not want to be left alone, but he felt he had been using Jenny in a way. Proposal first. Bed later.

He nodded bleakly and Jenny kissed him gently on the cheek, patted Towser, and went out.

Just then, the phone rang and he went to answer it. It was Jimmy Anderson, phoning from Strathbane. 'We've got the full confession,' he said cheerfully. 'Like to hear the rest?'

'Go ahead,' said Hamish.

'Well, to take the story up from where Mackay left off, he just smacked him on the back of the neck and Mainwaring toppled over into the tank. Mackay fled, taking the note with him. When he heard about the skeleton, he knew whose it was and how it got to be one, but he didn't know who had taken it out of the tank and cleaned up, see. He prayed that it might be some friendly local trying to cover up for the murderer, some local who wanted Mainwaring dead. Then Sandy turned up. Mackay had dropped his gold pen out of his jacket pocket when he'd bent over the tank as

Mainwaring sank. Sandy had taken the clothes and all the other bits and burned the things that would burn, chucked the false teeth on the moor, and thrown the watch in Loch Cnothan. He'd even shovelled up all the ash, put it in a sack with a brick, and sunk it in a peat bog.

'He wanted money. Mackay arranged to meet him up the river and when Sandy got there, Mackay waited until he had counted the money and put it in his jacket and then took out his trusty rusty pipe and clobbered Sandy the way he had clobbered Mainwaring and then he stuffed the body under a bush. Then he remembered the money. He wanted to go back and retrieve it, but found he couldn't bring himself to go near the corpse.'

'How are you going to keep it quiet about the lobsters?' asked Hamish.

'I don't know. Maybe Blair'll try to pervert the course of justice by saying, "Look, laddie, shut up about the lobsters and I'll see you get a lenient sentence," but I don't know. Who was the reporter who told you about the railway? That one in London?'

'It wasnae really a reporter,' said Hamish. 'It was my second cousin, who's a cleaning woman on the *Scottish Telegraph*. She reads everything she finds in the wastepaper buckets. She told me last year and I forgot about it until the other day. So Mainwaring in a way brought about his own death by deciding to interfere in Jamie's life. He left that glass of whisky on the tank, and Mackay got him when he went back to retrieve it. So it wasn't a cold-bloodedly planned murder; Mackay didn't leave the whisky for Sandy. The witchcraft had nothing to do with it . . . och, I suppose you'll be telling me next that that hoax call which got me out of the way was also made by someone else.'

'Aye. Mackay swears blind it wasnae him.'

'Alistair Gunn,' said Hamish suddenly. 'I'll bet it was Alistair Gunn. He was stinking o' fear when I arrived at The Clachan. He probably thought if the call was traced to him, then he would be charged with the murder. I gather they've released what's left of Mainwaring and the funeral's tomorrow.'

'Aye, are you going?'

'No,' said Hamish. 'I think I'll spend the day in bed. I found your murderer and I think I deserve a break.'

'You've got the luck o' the devil,' said Anderson. 'Cheery bye. Save me some whisky for your next murder.'

The shrilling of the telephone at seven the following morning dragged Hamish from his bed. He stumbled through to the office and picked it up. Blair's voice at the other end sounded almost obscenely cheerful.

'Great news, laddie,' he crowed. 'All our troubles are over.'

'What happened?' asked Hamish.

'Mackay hanged hisself in his cell last night. He can't talk and we can say what we like aboot the death.'

'So what's the official line?' asked Hamish.

'Oh, something like he cut off the flesh and threw it in the loch and then when he put the skeleton on the moor, the crows and buzzards and little wee foxes cleaned the rest – hence the scores on the bones. Sandy and the lobsters hasnae been mentioned.'

'Are ye sure it wass the suicide?' Hamish's voice was sharp.

There was a long silence and then Blair's voice sounded again, low and menacing this time. 'Jist you keep your long Highland nose oot o' this case. It's no longer got anything else to dae wi' you.' And then he banged down the receiver.

Hamish went through to get dressed. He felt sick. He kept seeing pictures in his head of a midnight visit to a cell and a prisoner being forcibly strung up.

When the phone rang again, he waited for a long time before going through and answering it. It was Jimmy Anderson.

'I've heard the news,' said Hamish bleakly.

'Aye, that's why I'm calling. Cheer up. He really did commit suicide. The pathologist confirmed it and he hates Blair and would have given anything to make it out to be murder if there had been the slightest doubt.'

Hamish let out a long sigh of relief. 'Thanks. Thanks a lot.'

Anderson chuckled. 'I know how much you love Blair and guessed what ye might be thinking. Ta-ta.'

Hamish Macbeth went straight back to bed and slept until noon.

Towser awoke him by tugging at his sleeve. 'Want a walk, boy?' mumbled Hamish. He had gone to bed the second time fully dressed. He got up and peered out of the window and found himself staring straight into a wall of snow.

Hamish groaned. 'I'd better dig a tunnel if I'm to get you out.'

The snow had stopped and by the time he had shovelled a path down to the gate, the sun was shining. He waited patiently while Towser cavorted among the snowdrifts. The snowplough chugged past as it had done before and threw a wall of snow up by the gate. 'Let it stay,' muttered Hamish. 'I don't feel like visitors the day.'

'Hello! Hamish Macbeth! Are you there?' called a voice from the other side of the snow wall. Jamie Ross.

'What is it?' called Hamish.

'Just want a wee word,' called Jamie. 'I'll shovel my end and you shovel yours and we might meet in the middle.'

Hamish sighed and picked up the shovel and dug until he had made a gap. He found Jamie and Helen Ross on the other side. 'Come in,' said Hamish reluctantly.

He led the way up the path and into the kitchen. Helen Ross looked more beautiful than ever in a white parka over a scarlet wool jump suit and white high boots.

'No more trouble, I hope?' asked Hamish.

'We felt we'd better give you an explanation,' said Jamie awkwardly. 'I told Helen to flirt with Mainwaring and find out if he knew about the plans for the railway.'

'So you knew about the plans?' asked Hamish.

'Yes. But not that they'd been cancelled.'

'It wasn't a very secret meeting,' said Hamish. 'I'm beginning to wonder if the whole of Sutherland knew about it.'

'Well, it turned out Mainwaring didn't have a clue about the railway, but he wasn't going to sell either.'

'Oh, well,' sighed Hamish. 'It's all over now. Why are you telling me this?'

'Helen didn't want you to think badly of her. That's why she spun you that tale about being bored and all.'

'I wish you had told me about the railway first thing,' said Hamish sharply. 'It would have saved a lot of time.'

He looked curiously at Helen as he spoke. She smiled at him and lit a cigarette. Hamish had a feeling that she had been telling the truth to a certain extent, that she had found Mainwaring's company a pleasure and had been disappointed with him in Inverness.

'And didn't you think you were doing anything wrong by risking your wife's reputation?' asked Hamish.

'Well, no,' said Jamie awkwardly. The fact that the whole thing had been Helen's idea hung in the air. 'But I tell you this, Hamish: I'll never do it again. I've been pushing and pushing to get money and more money, but I think greed and ambition are beginning to make me do things against my conscience. I'll need to start another business now, for when it comes out at the trial about those cannibalistic lobsters of mine, I'll be ruined.'

'It won't come out,' said Hamish. 'Mackay hanged himself last night.'

'Clever man,' said Helen Ross, and blew a smoke ring.

Jamie ignored her. 'Here!' he said. 'I hope it was suicide.'

'Yes, no doubt about it.'

Jamie looked dazed. 'I've been up all night,

plotting and planning what to do. Now I don't need to bother. But, you know, I can't help feeling heart-sorry for Mackay. I would have liked to murder Mainwaring myself. Well, we'd better be on our way.'

Hamish watched them as they picked their way down the path, Jamie holding his wife's arm so that she would not slip.

'It's a miracle he didn't murder Mainwaring,' said Hamish to Towser, 'for that man is married to a Lady Macbeth and disnae know it.'

Despite all his good intentions, Hamish found himself that evening in Jenny's cosy kitchen. She was flushed and excited and strangely guilty about something. He asked her what was wrong, but she blushed and said, 'Nothing.'

They had a pleasant dinner together and then went to bed for a more energetic night than they had had before.

Hamish awoke at dawn and propped himself up on one elbow and looked down at Jenny's flushed and sleeping face and at her black curls. He decided to ask her to marry him. The sick, unnatural yearning for Priscilla would soon go away. He lay back on the pillows and clasped his hands behind his head and wondered what Priscilla would think when she learned of his marriage. She would do the right thing, of course; she always did. She would congratulate him warmly and send him a suitable present. But when she came calling at his kitchen door in Lochdubh, she would be an intruder, no longer a friend. Perhaps he and Jenny would have children and he could buy them train sets and teach them how to fish. He drifted off to sleep again, and in his dream it was the day of his wedding to Jenny, and Priscilla was telling him she had always loved him.

He awoke with a groan. Jenny stirred and put an arm across his naked chest.

'Are you awake, Hamish?' she whispered.

'Yes,' said Hamish gloomily. He had to propose – now or never.

'There's something I've got to tell you.'

Both twisted round and stared at each other, for they had said the same thing at the same time.

'You first,' said Hamish.

'This is going to be difficult,' said Jenny. 'I love you, Hamish, but I'm going back to my husband.'

'I thought you were divorced?'

'I am. But this awful murder and Mainwaring insulting my painting suddenly made me realize I've never stopped loving Andrew. He phoned from Canada yesterday evening.

He still loves me, Hamish, and wants me back.'

Hamish at first felt a burst of sheer masculine fury, followed immediately by an odd floating feeling of relief.

'We're very good in bed together,' said Jenny in a small voice. 'But it's not enough, is it, Hamish?'

'No, I suppose not. When are you leaving?'

'Not for a few months. I've got to sell up here and start shipping my paintings and belongings to Canada. Hamish, are you mad at me? I shouldn't have gone to bed with you. But it just sort of happened.'

Jenny got out of bed and went to the window and drew the curtains. She scrubbed at the steamed-up glass with her fist and peered out. She shivered and crossed her arms over her naked breasts. 'It's snowing again, Hamish. What do you want to do?'

'Come back to bed and I'll show you,' said Hamish Macbeth.

The rest of Hamish's stay at Cnothan was quiet and dull. The snow changed to weeks of driving rain. He no longer made love to Jenny as lust on both sides disappeared, to be replaced by a comfortable friendship.

The first sunny morning in ages heralded his last day in Cnothan. He wanted to be out of the police station before MacGregor's return. He whistled as he cleaned the rooms and then he cleared all the groceries out of the kitchen cupboards and took them over to Jenny.

'MacGregor left me nothing,' said Hamish, 'so he can find things exactly the same on his return. There's three funny bottles of liqueur missing from his nasty bar, so I've left him a note, telling him to bill Blair.'

'I've made you some sandwiches and a Thermos of coffee for the bus,' said Jenny.

Hamish drew her into his arms and kissed her gently. 'I'll miss you, Jenny.'

She gave a little sniff and buried her head against his tunic. 'You can come and stay with us in Canada'

'No, Jenny. That would not be at all the thing. I'll drop you a line from time to time.'

'Here, I've a present for you.' Jenny went to the corner and picked up a large square parcel.

'What is it?' asked Hamish.

'It's that painting of Clachan Mohr I did when I was angry.'

'You could get a lot of money for that, Jenny,' said Hamish awkwardly. 'Or you could take it to your husband. He'd never call you a chocolate-box painter again.'

'He's admitted he was jealous,' said Jenny cheerfully. 'He really knows my paintings are good. I really don't like that one, Hamish.'

'Well, I'll take it,' said Hamish. But he privately thought it was a pity that Jenny did not realize her ex-soon-to-be non-ex husband had been right in the first place and was probably only being tactful now.

The small Lochdubh bus came screeching to a halt outside the post office as he stood there an hour later with his bags, his painting, and his dog.

The driver threw him an evil look and went off to buy cigarettes.

Hamish climbed on the bus, put his luggage on one seat and sat on the other with Towser beside him. The whole town was swimming in lazy golden light and people walked up and down aimlessly, looking drugged in the unfamiliar warmth.

A car drew to a halt beside the bus. Hamish looked idly down at the driver who was climbing out and his heart gave a painful lurch. Priscilla Halburton-Smythe. He stared straight ahead, his heart racing.

She poked her head in the door of the bus. 'Want a lift to Lochdubh, copper?' she called. Towser threw himself on Priscilla, uttering ecstatic yips of welcome.

'Aye, that'll be grand, Priscilla,' said Hamish, his eyes wary.

He tried not to look at her, but was painfully aware of slim, stylish elegance and golden hair.

He wrestled with his bags and painting and climbed down from the bus. Priscilla opened the boot. 'Put your bags in there, Hamish,' she said. 'What's that parcel? It looks like a painting.'

'It is,' said Hamish. 'I'd better put it in the back seat so it disnae get damaged.'

'Won't Towser sit on it?'

'No, he'll sleep on the floor. You know that, Priscilla.'

'Yes, I know that.' She straightened up after arranging his bags in the boot and slammed down the lid. Her eyes were clear and untroubled but slightly questioning.

'You haven't given me much of a welcome,' she said.

'I'm glad to see you,' said Hamish formally. Then he went and climbed into the passenger seat, after putting Towser and the painting in the back of the car.

Priscilla was about to drive off when she suddenly switched off the engine and said, 'There's some woman running towards us. Do you know her?'

'It's Jenny,' said Hamish. He rolled down the window.

'I'm glad I caught you,' panted Jenny. 'You

214

forgot your sandwiches and Thermos.' She peered across Hamish at Priscilla.

'Priscilla, this is Jenny Lovelace. Jenny, Priscilla Halburton-Smythe.'

Priscilla reached across Hamish and shook hands. Then Jenny blushed furiously. 'Oh, I've put oil paint on your hand. I'm so sorry.'

'It's all right,' said Priscilla, opening her handbag and taking out a packet of tissues and a bottle. 'I have some nail varnish remover that will take it off.'

She would, thought Hamish glumly.

'Can . . . can I have a word in private with you, Hamish?' asked Jenny.

Hamish slid out of the car. Priscilla watched as Jenny said something and then threw her arms around Hamish's tall figure and hugged him fiercely. Priscilla felt silly and miserable and wished she had not come. She had phoned Cnothan and had learned Hamish was leaving that day. A woman had answered the phone in the police station. Probably Jenny.

'That must have been who phoned yesterday when you were out,' whispered Jenny. 'I forgot to tell you. Sorry.'

'It's all right, Jenny. Goodbye. Write to me.'

Hamish climbed back in the car. Jenny's eyes filled with tears, and she turned and ran away up the main street.

Priscilla let in the clutch, and the Volvo moved off smoothly. She was wearing a tailored tweed jacket, worn open over a white shirt, with a slim heather wool skirt and sheer tights ending in sensible brogues. The bell of her fair hair fell smoothly on either side of the classic oval of her face.

'I came because I was feeling sorry for you,' said Priscilla. 'Cnothan is not my favourite place. But you appear to have been happy here.'

Hamish grunted and folded his arms.

'Who is she?'

'Local artist.'

'That her painting you've got in the back?'

'Yes.'

Priscilla drew to a stop outside Cnothan Game. 'I'd like to see it,' she said.

'Go ahead,' said Hamish. At that moment, he didn't care what she did. She had no right to barge coolly back into his life and open up all the old wounds.

Priscilla opened the parcel carefully and then studied the painting for a long time.

'Poor Jenny,' she said. 'The murder must have been an awful experience.'

Hamish felt a sudden rush of affection for Priscilla, for that quick sensitivity of hers that was so often masked by the sophisticated outward appearance.

'She's all right now,' he said, as Priscilla replaced the painting and climbed back into the driver's seat. 'She's going back to Canada to remarry her husband.'

Priscilla shot him a look. She felt light-hearted and happy.

At that moment, Helen Ross came strolling out into the yard of Cnothan Game. She was wearing a leaf-green wool mini that exposed miles of sheer-stockinged leg. She swayed towards them.

'Drive on,' said Hamish urgently.

'Looks like the local siren,' said Priscilla, speeding off.

'More like the local Lady Macbeth.'

'Lady ... Oh, I see. For a moment I thought ... Never mind. Look, let's go up on the moors and eat some of Jenny's sandwiches. I'm starving.'

Soon they were sitting on top of a rise over-looking Cnothan.

'Out of the Valley of the Shadow of Death,' said Hamish.

'You had a nightmare of a time, didn't you, Hamish?' said Priscilla, pouring coffee and opening up packets of sandwiches. 'Tell me about it.'

Hamish talked and talked while Priscilla listened. He found himself telling her about the strange atmosphere of Cnothan, about how he kept losing his temper, about the murder, but not about the lobsters. The more he talked, the lighter and happier he felt. He could feel his old lazy, easygoing self returning.

When they drove off, the bond of friendship was restored, and along with it the old seductive feeling of not being alone in the world any longer, the relief of being able to communicate to someone who knew exactly what you were thinking and feeling.

But as they neared Lochdubh, Priscilla broke off from a long description of the irritations and boredoms of the hat shop to say crossly, 'What are you thinking of, Hamish Macbeth? You stopped listening to me exactly five minutes ago.'

'I was wondering, Priscilla . . . did you eat any lobster when you were in London?'

'Did I . . .? Sometimes I think you are just plain mad, Hamish Macbeth. Oh, I know what it is, you're scrounging again. Very well, you win. Priscilla shall cook Hamish a lobster for his dinner.'

'Oh, no,' said Hamish with a shudder. 'I cannae thole the beasts.'

Priscilla slowed the car to a halt and looked at Hamish. She remembered seeing Hamish eat lobster thermidor at the Lochdubh Hotel with great relish. There was a blackness emanating from Hamish. Skeleton, she thought suddenly. Mainwaring was killed at Cnothan Game and Fish Company. Jamie Ross was famous for his lobsters. Scratches on the skeleton.

She put a hand on his knee.

'We'll never eat lobster again, Hamish'

Hamish let out a long sigh. 'Quick on the uptake, aren't you? I'd forgotten that.'

'Dinner at the Lochdubh on me,' said Priscilla firmly. 'They do a very good vegetarian salad.

If you enjoyed *Death of an Outsider*, read on for the first chapter of the next book in the *Hamish Macbeth* series . . .

DEATH of a PERFECT WIFE

Chapter One

'Will you walk into my parlour?' said a
spider to a fly: 'Tis the prettiest little
parlour that ever you did spy.'
                                   – Mary Howitt

It was another day like the morning of the
world.

Police Constable Hamish Macbeth, his dog
at his heels, sauntered along the waterfront of
Lochdubh, a most contented man. For two
whole weeks the weather had been perfect.

Above was a cerulean sky and before him
the bustling little harbour, and beyond that the
blue of the sea, incredible blue, flashing with
diamonds as the sun sparkled on the choppy
surface of the water. Around the village rose
the towering mountains of Sutherland, the
oldest in the world, benign in the lazy light.
Across the sea loch was Gray Forest, a cool
dark cathedral of tall straight pines. Early
roses tumbled over garden fences and sweet

peas fluttered their Edwardian beauty in the faintest of breezes. On the flanks of the mountains, bell heather, the early heather that blossoms in June, coloured the green and brown camouflage of the rising moors with splashes of deepest pink. Hairbells, the bluebells of Scotland, trembled at the roadside among the blazing twisted yellow and purple of vetch and the white trumpets of convolvulus.

As Hamish strolled along, he noticed the Currie sisters, Jessie and Nessie, two of Lochdubh's spinsters, tending their little patch of garden. The garden bore a regimented look. The flowers were in neat rows behind an edging of shells.

'Fine day,' said Hamish, smiling over the hedge. Both sisters straightened up from weeding a flower bed and surveyed the constable with disfavour.

'Nothing to do as usual, I suppose,' said Nessie severely, the sunlight sparkling on her thick glasses.

'And isn't that the best thing?' said Hamish cheerfully. 'No crime, no battered wives, and not even a drunk to lock up.'

'Then the police station should be closed down. The police station should be closed down,' said Jessie, who repeated everything twice over like the brave thrush. 'It's a sin and a shame to see a well-built man lazing about. A sin and a shame.'

'Och, I'll find a murder jist for you,' said Hamish, 'and then you really will have something to complain about.'

'I hear Miss Halburton-Smythe is back,' said Jessie, peering maliciously at the constable. 'She's brought some of her friends from London to stay.'

'Good time to come here,' said Hamish amiably. 'Lovely weather.'

He smiled and touched his cap and strolled on, but the smile left his face as soon as he was out of sight. Priscilla Halburton-Smythe was the love of his life. He wondered when she had come back and who was with her. He wondered when he would see her. Anxiety began to cast a cloud over his mind. It seemed amazing that the day was still perfect: the sun still shone and a seal rolled about lazily in the calm waters of the bay.

He tried to recover his spirits. The air smelled of salt and tar and pine. He walked on to the Lochdubh Hotel to see if he could scrounge a cup of coffee.

Mr Johnson, the manager, was in his office when Hamish walked in. 'Help yourself,' he said with a jerk of his head towards the coffee machine in the corner. He waited until Hamish was seated over a cup of coffee and said, 'The Willets's place has been sold.'

Hamish raised his eyebrows. 'I wouldnae hae thought anyone would have taken that.'

The Willets's house was a Victorian villa set back from the waterfront. It had been up for sale for five years and was in bad repair.

'I gather they got it for a song. Someone said ten thousand pounds was the figure.'

'And who's they?'

'Name of Thomas. English. Don't know anything about them. Expected to move in today. Maybe it'll be work for you.'

Hamish grinned. 'A crime, you mean? With weather like this, nothing bad can happen.'

'The glass is falling.'

'I never knew a barometer yet that could tell the weather,' said Hamish. 'What's happening up at Tommel Castle?' Hamish asked the question with a casual air of indifference, but Mr Johnson was not deceived. Tommel Castle, some miles outside Lochdubh, was the home of Priscilla Halburton-Smythe.

'I gather Priscilla's come back with a party of friends,' said the manager.

Hamish took a sip of coffee. 'What kind of friends?'

'Sloane Rangers, I think. Two fellows and two girls.'

Hamish was conscious of a feeling of relief. It sounded like two couples. He dreaded to hear that Priscilla had brought a boyfriend with her.

'Had a look at them yet?' he asked.

'Oh, aye, they were in for dinner here last night.'

Hamish stiffened. 'And what has happened to the colonel's hospitality when his daughter has to entertain her friends at the local hotel?'

Mr Johnson looked uncomfortable. 'They've been at the castle for over a week,' he said, and then looked at the ceiling so that he should not see the disappointment in Hamish's eyes.

Hamish put his unfinished coffee slowly down on the desk. 'I'd better be getting off on my rounds,' he said. 'Come along, Towser.' The big mongrel slouched out after his master, his plume of a tail at half-mast as if he sensed Hamish's distress.

Hamish stood out in the forecourt of the hotel among the tubs of scarlet geraniums and blinked in the sunlight. It seemed strange that the weather was still as glorious as ever. Over a week! And she had not called.

He went to the police station and then through the garden at the back and up to his small croft to make sure his sheep had enough water. The sun was hot on his back, curlews piped from the heather and overhead a buzzard, like Icarus, sailed straight for the sun.

A large black ewe ambled up and nuzzled his hand. Hamish automatically patted the sheep, his thoughts on what was going on at the castle. Priscilla had said something teasing last time before she had left about his lazy lack of ambition. He was certainly not an ambitious man. He enjoyed his easygoing life and he loved western Sutherland with its mountains and heather and the broad stretch of the Atlantic beyond the sea loch where the old people said the blue men rode the waves and the dead came back as seals.

He decided it would do no harm just to go up to the castle and have a look.

He had a new white Land Rover, a perk from head office in Strathbane, no doubt with the blessing of Chief Detective Inspector Blair who enjoyed a reputation for solving murders with Hamish's help, even though Hamish had solved them single-handedly but had let the boorish detective take the credit.

The twisting road up to the castle wound through the hills and his heart lifted as the road bore him higher above the village. There would be some simple explanation as to why Priscilla had not been to see him. Her father, the colonel, strongly disapproved of her friendship with the local bobby. He had probably told her not to have anything to do with him, though Hamish, deliberately forgetting that her father's temper and disapproval had not stopped Priscilla from visiting him in the past.

He parked the Land Rover on the verge outside the gates. He wanted to spy out the lie of the land before he was seen.

He walked slowly up the drive. He could hear shouts and laughter, so instead of following round the turn of the drive that would bring him to the lawns in front of the house, he plunged into the pine wood at the side and made his way silently over the pine needles to where he could get a clear view without being seen himself.

They were playing croquet, Priscilla and her friends. At first, he had eyes only for her. She was bent over the mallet, the golden bell of her hair falling about her face. She was wearing a plain white blouse, a short straight scarlet cotton skirt, and low-heeled brown sandals with thin straps. Hamish's attention turned to the man who had come up to her and put his arms around her to show her how to use the mallet. He was tall, with crisp dark hair, a handsome face, and a blue chin. He was wearing a checked shirt and black curling hairs sprouted at the open neck. His sleeves were rolled up, revealing strong tanned arms covered with black hair.

There were two girls, both with the monkey faces of rich Chelsea, and well-coiffed hair. They were wearing casual clothes. The other man was a rabbity-looking individual with gold-rimmed glasses.

Then as Hamish watched, Priscilla smiled at the dark-haired man, a radiant smile, a happy smile, and Hamish felt cold. A darkness grew inside him. Priscilla Halburton-Smythe was in love with that hairy ape, that Neanderthal. His distress was sharp and acute. Suddenly, the smile left Priscilla's face and she looked about her and then at the trees.

Hamish crept silently away. He felt numb. Misery dragged at his feet like clay as he walked back to the Land Rover.

He drove very carefully back to Lochdubh, drove like a drunk man trying to sober up.

Then he saw a large dusty removal van outside the Willets's house. The newcomers had arrived.

Rather than be alone with himself and his thoughts, Hamish drove straight to the house and parked beside the van. A couple, a tall, rather elegant woman and a big shambling man, were unloading bits and pieces.

'Need any help?' he asked. 'I'm Hamish Macbeth, the local bobby.'

The woman wiped her hand on her trousers and held it out. 'Trixie Thomas,' she said, 'and this is my husband, Paul.'

She was almost as tall as Hamish. She had long brown hair which curled naturally on her shoulders and brown eyes, very large with bluish whites. Her mouth was thin and her teeth, rather prominent when she smiled, very white. Hamish judged her to be about forty-five. Her husband, a large bear of a man with a crumpled clown's face, looked like a fat man who had recently been on a severe diet. His skin looked baggy as if it was meant to stretch across a fatter frame. He had little black eyes and a big mouth and a squashed nose.

'Are you managing?' asked Hamish.

'We're doing our best,' sighed Trixie. 'But it *is* hot. We rented this removal van. Couldn't afford the professionals so I suppose we'll have to manage . . . somehow.' Her eyes grew wider and her mouth drooped and her hands fluttered in a helpless gesture.

'I'll give you a hand,' said Hamish. He removed his peaked cap and rolled up the sleeves of his blue regulation shirt.

'Oh, *would* you?' breathed Trixie. 'Poor Paul is so *helpless*.' She had a breathless sort of voice, marred by a faint Cockney whine.

Hamish glanced at Paul to see how he liked being described as helpless but the big man was smiling amiably.

Glad of something to take his mind off his troubles, Hamish worked steadily. He and Paul loaded in the furniture and the bric-a-brac and books while Trixie walked about the house showing them where to put things. 'We'll need more furniture,' she said. 'We're both on the dole and we decided to turn this into a bed and breakfast.'

'Aye, well, if you're quick about it, you might get the tourists for July and August,' said Hamish. 'And if you want any second-hand stuff, there's a good place over at Alness. It's a bit of a drive . . .'

Trixie's mouth drooped again. 'We haven't a penny left for furniture,' she said. 'I was hoping some of the locals might have some bits and pieces they don't want.'

'Maybe I've got something I can let you have,' said Hamish. 'When we've finished, come over to the station and I'll make you something to eat.'

He regretted the invitation as soon as it was out of his mouth. Although by no means a vain man, he had a feeling Trixie was making a pass at him. She was emanating a sort of come-hither sexiness, occasionally bumping into him as if by accident, and giving him a slow smile.

He regretted his invitation even more when the couple arrived at the police station. While he was cooking in the kitchen, Trixie wandered off into the other rooms without asking permission and was soon back, her face a little flushed and her eyes wider than ever. 'I notice you don't use the fire,' she said, 'and there's that old coal scuttle. We don't have a coal scuttle.' She smiled ruefully. 'Couldn't afford one.'

The coal scuttle had been given to Hamish by an aunt. It was an old eighteenth-century one with enamelled panels and he was very fond of it. Her eyes seemed to be swallowing him up and he was surprised at the effort it took to shake his head and say, 'No, I use that the whole time in the winter. You cannae expect me to light fires in a heat wave.'

Trixie was now examining the contents of the kitchen shelves. She lifted down a pot of homemade jam and examined the label. 'Strawberry! Just look, Paul. And homemade. I love homemade jam.'

'Take it with you when you go,' said Hamish. She threw her arms around him. 'Isn't he delightful?' she said.

Hamish extricated himself and served the meal on the kitchen table.

He was beginning to dislike Trixie but he did not yet know why that dislike should be so intense. He turned his attention to Paul. The big man said they had decided to get out of the rat race and come north to the Highlands and maybe earn their living taking in paying guests. 'There's a lot to be done to the house,' he said, 'but it shouldn't take too long to fix, and then I thought I might start a market garden. There's a good bit of garden there.'

'The trouble is,' said Hamish, moving his long legs to one side to avoid Trixie's, which had been pressing against his own, 'that the summers haven't been very good and people have been taking holidays abroad. Mind you, with all the jams at the airports, they were saying on the news that people are starting to holiday in Britain again so you might be lucky.'

'We put advertisements already in the *Glasgow Herald* and *The Scotsman*, advertising accommodation for July and August,' said Trixie.

Hamish thought that for a pair with little money it was odd that they had found enough to advertise. And it was nearly the end of June. They would need to work very hard to get the rooms ready in time.

When they stood up to go, Trixie said, 'I don't want to be a pest, but if you've any little thing in the way of furniture . . .? I mean, it's all paid for by the government anyway.'

'Only the desk and chair, filing cabinet, and phone in the office are supplied by the police force,' said Hamish. 'The living quarters are all furnished by me. I haven't time to look at the rooms at the moment, but if I find anything, I'll let you know.'

With a feeling of relief, he ushered them out. It was only when he was watching them make their way back to their own house that he realized with something of a shock that the weather had changed. The air felt damp and there was a thin veil of cloud covering the sun. He walked slowly round the front of the police station and stared down the loch.

Rain clouds were heading in from the sea on a damp wind. They were trailing long fingers over the water that had a black oily swell.

And then the midges came down, those Scottish mosquitoes, the plague of the Highlands. All during the long, dry spell, they had been mercifully absent. Now they descended in clouds, getting in his eyes and up his nose. He ran back into the kitchen, cursing, and shut the door.

The idyll was over. The weather had broken, Priscilla had returned with a man, and that couple had moved into Lochdubh, bringing with them an atmosphere of unease and trouble to come.

That evening, Dr Brodie settled down to a large dinner of steak and chips. He and his wife ate at the round kitchen table. He had long ago given up any hope of ever finding it clear. His plate was surrounded by books and magazines and tapes and unanswered letters. The fruit bowl in front of him contained paper clips, hairpins, two screwdrivers, a tube of glue, and a withered orange.

His wife was sitting opposite him, a book propped up against the wine bottle. Dr Brodie surveyed her with affection. She had a thin intelligent face and large grey eyes. Wispy fair hair as fine as a baby's fell across her face and she put up a coal-smeared hand to brush it away. Dr Brodie was a contented man. He enjoyed his small practice in the village and although he sometimes wished his wife, Angela, were a better housekeeper, he had become accustomed to his messy, cluttered home. Angela's two spaniels snored under the table and the cat promenaded on top.

'The cat's just walked across your plate,' commented the doctor.

'Oh, did it? *Shoo!*' said Angela, absent-mindedly, waving a hand and then turning another page of her book.

'There are new people at the Willets's place,' said the doctor, pouring brown sauce over his steak and ketchup over his chips. He pulled away the wine bottle and poured himself a glass. Angela's book fell over.

'I said there are new people at the Willets's place,' repeated her husband.

His wife's dreamy eyes focussed on him. 'I suppose I had better go and welcome them tomorrow,' she said. 'I'll bake them a cake.'

'You'll what? When could you ever bake a cake?'

Angela sighed. 'I'm not a very good house-keeper, am I? But on this occasion, I am going to be good. I bought a packet of cake mix. I can simply follow the instructions.'

'Suit yourself. Priscilla Halburton-Smythe called down at the surgery to pick up a prescription for her father. She drove straight off afterwards.'

'And?'

'Well, she's been back over a week and she hasn't called at the police station once.'

'Poor Hamish. Why does he bother? He's an attractive man.'

'Priscilla's a very beautiful girl.'

'Yes, isn't she,' said Angela in a voice which held no trace of envy. 'Maybe I'll bake a cake for Hamish, too.'

'The fire extinguisher's above the stove, remember,' cautioned her husband. 'The time you tried to make jam, everything went up in flames.'

'It won't happen again,' said Angela. 'I must have been thinking about something else.'

She rose to her feet and opened the fridge door and took out two glass dishes of trifle which she had bought that day at the bakery. The trifle consisted of rubbery custard, thin red jam, and ersatz cream. The doctor ate it with enjoyment and washed it down with Chianti and then lit a cigarette.

He was in his fifties, a slim, dapper little man with a balding head, light blue eyes, a freckled face, and dressed in shabby tweeds that he wore winter and summer.

After dinner, the couple moved through to the living room while the cat roamed over the kitchen table, sniffing at the dirty plates.

The fire had gone out. Angela never raked out the ashes until the fireplace became so full of them that the fire would not light. She knelt down in front of the hearth and began to shovel out piles of grey ash into a bucket.

'Why bother?' said the doctor. 'Light the electric fire.'

'Good idea,' said Angela. She rose to her feet, leaving ash all over the hearth and plugged in the fire and switched it on. Despite the warm weather, their house was always cold. It was an old cottage with thick walls and stone floors. Angela then went back to the table, absent-mindedly patted the cat, picked up her book, returned to the living room, and began to read again.

The doctor had learned to live with his wife's messy housekeeping. He would have been very surprised could he have known that Angela often felt she could not bear it any longer.

Often she thought of getting down to it and giving the place a thoroughly good clean, but a grey depression would settle on her. For relaxation she had once enjoyed reading women's magazines but now she could not even bear to look at one, the glossy pictures of perfect kitchens and fresh net curtains making her feel desperately inadequate.

But on the following morning after she had served up her husband's breakfast – fried black pudding, haggis, bacon, sausages, fried bread and two eggs – she felt a lifting of her heart. She had a Purpose. She would behave as a good wife should and bake a cake and take it over to the new neighbours.

When she settled down to read the instructions on the back of the packet of Joseph's Ready Mix, she experienced a strong feeling of resentment. If it was indeed a 'ready mix' then why did she have to add eggs and milk and salt and all these fiddly things that should have been in the packet already?

She searched around for the cake tin and then remembered the dogs were using it as a drinking bowl. She threw out the water and put the dogs' water in a soup bowl instead, wiped out the cake tin with a paper towel, greased it, and started to work.

That afternoon, she set out for the Willets's place – no, Thomas's place, she reminded herself – feeling very proud of herself. She held in front of her, like a crown on a cushion, a sponge cake filled with cream.

There seemed to be a lot of activity around the old Victorian villa. Archie Maclean, one of the local fishermen, was carrying in a small table, Mrs Wellington, the minister's wife, was cleaning the windows, and Bert Hook, a crofter, was up on the roof, clearing out the gutters.

The front door was open, and Angela walked inside. A tall woman approached her. 'My name's Trixie Thomas,' she said. 'Oh, what a beautiful cake. We adore cake, but what with us being unemployed and living on government handouts, we've had to cut out luxuries like this.'

Angela introduced herself and felt a rush of pride when Trixie said, 'In fact, we're ready for a coffee break. We'll have it now.'

She led the way into the kitchen. Her husband, Paul, was washing down the walls. 'All the poor dear's fit for,' said Trixie in a rueful aside. She raised her voice, 'Darling, here's the doctor's wife with a delicious cake. We'll take a break and have some coffee. Sit down, Angela.'

Angela sat down at a table covered with a bright red-and-white checked gingham cloth. Bluebottles buzzed against the window. 'You should get a spray,' said Angela. 'The flies are dreadful today.'

'I think there's been enough damage to the ozone layer already,' said Trixie. 'What I need are some old-fashioned fly papers.'

She was making coffee in what looked like a brand-new machine. 'I grind my own beans,' she said over her shoulder. Paul was already seated at the table, looking at the cake like a greedy child. 'Now, just a small piece, mind,' cautioned his wife. 'You're on a diet.'

Angela watched Trixie with admiration. Trixie was wearing a sort of white linen smock with large pockets over blue jeans and sneakers. Her sneakers were snow white without even a grass stain on them. Angela tugged miserably at her crumpled blouse, which had ridden up over the waistband of her baggy skirt, and felt messy and grubby.

'Now, for the cake,' said Trixie, bringing out a knife. Paul hunched over the table, waiting eagerly.

The knife sank into the cake. Trixie tried to lift out a slice. It was uncooked in the middle. A yellowy sludge oozed out.

'Oh, dear,' said Angela. 'You can't eat that. I don't know how that could have happened. I followed the instructions on the packet so carefully.'

'It's all right,' said Paul quickly. 'I'll eat it.'

'No, you won't,' said Trixie, giving Angela a conspiratorial 'men!' sort of smile.

'I'm hopeless,' mourned Angela.

'Don't worry. I'll show you how to make one. It's just as easy to make a cake from scratch as it is with one of these packets. And it was a lovely thought.' Trixie moved the cake out of her husband's reach. He gave a sigh and lumbered to his feet and went back to work.

'I can't do anything right,' said Angela. 'I am utterly useless about the house. It's like a rubbish bin.'

'You've probably let it go too far,' said Trixie with quick sympathy. 'Why don't you get someone in to clean?'

'Oh, I couldn't. You see, it's so awful, I'd need to make a start on it myself before any cleaning woman could see what she was doing.'

'I'll help you,' Trixie smiled at Angela. 'I feel we are going to be friends.'

Angela coloured up and turned briefly away to hide the look of embarrassed gratification on her face. She had never fitted in very well with the women of the village. In fact, she had never talked to anyone before about how she felt about her dirty house. 'I really couldn't expect you to help me, Trixie,' said Angela, feeling quite modern and bold because people in the village called each other by their sur-names, Mr or Mrs This and That, until they had known each other for years.

'I'll strike a bargain with you,' said Trixie. 'I'll nip back to your house with you and if you can let me have any old sticks of furniture you were thinking of throwing out, I'll take that as payment.'

'Lovely,' said Angela with a comfortable feeling she had not experienced since a child of being taken in hand.

But as they walked to the doctor's house, Angela began to wish she had not let Trixie come. She thought of the ash still spilling over the hearth on to the carpet and of all the sinister grease lurking in the kitchen.

Trixie strode in, rolling up her sleeves. She walked from room to room downstairs and then said briskly, 'Now, the best thing to do is just get started and don't think about anything else.'

And Trixie worked. Her hands flew here and here. She was amazingly competent. Grease disappeared, surfaces began to gleam, books flew back up on the shelves. It was all magic to Angela, who felt she was watching a sort of Mary Poppins at work. She blundered around after her new mentor, cheerfully doing everything she was instructed to do as if the house were Trixie's and not her own.

'Well, we've made a start,' said Trixie at last.

'A start!' Angela was amazed. 'It's never been so clean. I just don't know how to thank you.'

'Perhaps you've got an old piece of furniture you don't want?'

'Of course.' Angela looked about her helplessly. 'There must be something somewhere.'

'What about that old chair in the corner of your living room?'

'You mean that thing?' The chair was armless with a bead-and-needlework cover.

Angela hesitated only a moment. It had been her grandmother's but no one ever sat on it and her gratitude for this new goddess of the household was immense. 'Yes, I'll get John to put it in the station wagon and run it over to you this evening.'

'No need for that.' Trixie lifted it in strong arms. 'I'll carry it.'

Despite Angela's protests that it was too heavy for her, Trixie headed off. Angela followed her to the garden gate. She wanted to say, 'When will I see you again?' and felt as shy as a lover. Dr Brodie was often away on calls and she spent much of her life alone. She had never worked since the day of her marriage to the young medical student, John Brodie, thirty years ago. They had been unable to have children. Angela's parents were dead. She felt she had somehow only managed to muddle through the years of her marriage with books as her only consolation.

Trixie turned at the gate. 'See you tomorrow,' she said.

Angela grinned, her thin face youthful and happy.

'See you tomorrow,' she echoed.

Constable Hamish Macbeth was leaning on his garden gate as Trixie went past, carrying the chair.

'Need any help?' he called.

'No, thanks,' said Trixie, hurrying past.

Hamish looked at her retreating figure. Where had he seen that chair? His mind ranged over the interiors of the houses in Lochdubh. The doctor's! That was it.

He ambled along the road to the doctor's house and went around to the side, no one in the Highlands except the Thomas's bothering to use the front door.

'Come in, Hamish,' called Angela, seeing the lanky figure of the red-haired policeman lurking in the doorway. 'Like a cup of coffee?'

'Yes, please.' Hamish eased himself into the kitchen, and then blinked in surprise. He had never seen the Brodies' kitchen look so clean. Angela bubbled over with enthusiasm as she told him of Trixie's help.

'Was that your chair she was carrying?' asked Hamish.

'Yes, the poor things have very little furniture. They want to start a bed-and-breakfast place. It was just a tatty old thing of my grandmother's.'

Hamish thought quickly. Someone setting up a bed-and-breakfast establishment usually wanted old serviceable stuff. He wondered uneasily whether the chair was valuable. But he did not know anything about antiques.

Flies buzzed about the kitchen.

'I should have kept the door shut,' said Angela. 'Wretched flies.'

'You've got a spray there,' pointed out Hamish.

'These sprays make holes in the ozone layer,' said Angela.

'I suppose so. But it's hard to think of the environment when you haff the kitchen full of the beasties,' said Hamish whose Highland voice became more sibilant when he was upset, and somehow he felt that that remark about the ozone layer originally came from Trixie. And yet Trixie was right, so why should he feel so resentful?

After some gossip, Hamish got up and left. A thin drizzle was falling. The sky was weeping over the loch, but the air was warm and clammy.

And then he saw a Volvo parked at the side of the police station and Priscilla just getting out of it. He broke into a run.